To Tony
Thanks for your
Nandi 10/8/0?

THE TRUE NANNY DIARIES

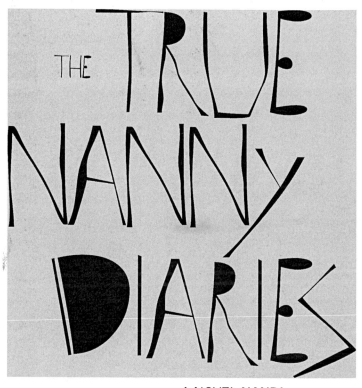

THE TRUE NANNY DIARIES

A NOVEL **NANDI**

Bread
for ≡
Brick
Brooklyn, NY

Published by Bread for Brick, Brooklyn, New York
info@breadforbrickpublishing.com
www.breadforbrickpublishing.com
347-636-0079

Publisher's Note
This is a work of fiction. Names, characters, places and events are either the product of the author's imagination or are used fictitiously. Any resemblance to real people, living or dead, incidents, or locales is strictly coincidental.

LIBRARY OF CONGRESS CONTROL NO: 2008910763

NANDI
The True Nanny Diaries / Nandi
ISBN: 978-0-615-22060-4

Printed in the United States of America
Set in ITC Franklin Gothic and DrunkPoet
Cover design by Blondie Brodhurst
Cover concept by Omidiran Khali Kwodwo Keyi-Ogunlade
Interior and chapter titling by Michael L. Lawrence/MasTypography Studio
Author's photograph by Danella Abbey

To my daughter
Kenya Nsoromma: Star from the heavens

"There will come a time when you believe everything is finished.
  That will be the beginning."

— *Louis L'Amour*

The "True" Nanny Experience

State Senator Kevin Parker (D-NY), 21st Senate District, Brooklyn

AS A CONSISTENT SUPPORTER OF IMMIGRANTS' RIGHTS, I enthusiastically support this seminal work by Nandi. We are fortunate that one stride from her dance with destiny placed her in the role of a domestic worker. It is from her vantage point at ground zero of this "invisible world" that we gain this colorful, fictionalized work, *The True Nanny Diaries*. A brilliant writer and an experienced journalist, Nandi delineates, with humor and compassion, the grinding demands on the lives of domestic workers that is candid as it is crafty. But, *The True Nanny Diaries* is not only about the challenges of the workplace, but about the hopes, dreams and aspirations that domestic workers have for themselves and their own families. Nandi reminds us that real people exist behind the mops and the strollers. They, too, deserve all the legal protections afforded to other American workers.

The True Nanny Diaries points up a glaringly embarrassing truth: domestic workers are purposefully excluded from basic, legal protections that cover other American workers. Historically, domestic workers are not protected by many state laws, as are workers in other industries. Thus, they are legally excluded from the National Labor Relations Act (NLRA). This prevents them from organizing labor unions for the purpose of collective bargaining. When Franklin D. Roosevelt signed the NLRA in 1935, *pressure from Southern Democrats pushed him to exclude agricultural and domestic work, both professions with strong roots in enslavement that were still predominantly held by African Americans at the time (The American Prospect).* Thus, employers are not required to pay overtime or grant maternity leave. Wage standards, sick days and advance notice of termination are at the employers' discretion. Also, they are not obliged to provide health insurance, though domestic work is often physically demanding and sometimes dangerous. Further, many domestic workers are women of color who, because of race and gender discrimination, are particularly vulnerable to unfair labor practices.

Here, in New York State, many organizations, in particular, Domestic Workers United, have worked tirelessly on the creation and passage of the Domestic Workers' Bill of Rights (Senate Bill S2311) of which I am a sponsor. The Bill, introduced in 2004, is currently winding its way through the legislative process. If passed, it will amend New York State's labor law to give thousands of housekeepers, nannies and companions to the elderly, inter alia, one day off each calendar week, seven days of sick leave and five vacation days each year. It would include domestic workers and their employers in the New York State human rights law.

I cannot overstate the importance of this legislation. According to statistics compiled between 2003–2004 by Domestic Workers United, the Brennan Center for Justice at New York University and the New York-based Jews for Racial and Economic Justice, there are approximately 200,000 domestic workers employed in New York State. Twenty-six percent earn wages below the poverty line; fifty percent work overtime — ten to 20 hours above the normal workweek — but only 30 percent earn overtime pay. These agencies find that 90 percent have no health insurance from their employers. Clearly, these workers, who are charged with protecting society's young and frail, are vulnerable themselves.

Although the labor of approximately 1.5 million nannies, maids, and housekeepers is still central to the ongoing prosperity of this nation, they remain among the most marginalized in the United States. This situation persists, despite the centrality of their contribution to the most important element of their employers' lives: caring for their families, children and homes. Because the ongoing oppression of domestic workers has largely been created from federal law, I am making the call for a National Domestic Workers' Bill of Rights, to raise the living standards of all domestic workers in America.

As the world of *The True Nanny Diaries* underscores, many domestic workers in America are undocumented immigrants who, working at the margins of legality, constantly fear deportation. Senate Bill S2311 will not change much for this category of worker and sadly, long after its passage, they will continue to exist beyond its reach. I believe that passage of Senate Bill S2311 must serve as a challenge to engage comprehensive immigration reform and create a pathway to citizenship for them. It is imperative that we protect these workers who, though undocumented, give their all so that Americans can conduct their own important work outside of the home. In this context, a Domestic Workers' Bill of Rights is only fire on the ice of the larger, complex and often controversial issue of immigration.

Though a land of immigrants, it is clear that America has not always received the foreign-born with open arms. Twenty-three years after the 1986 overhaul of immigration laws offered amnesty to seven million undocumented immigrants, up to 10 million people are still without papers. As chairman of the New York State Senate Task Force on New Americans, I am impassioned about the possibilities of making the American Dream an attainable reality for millions of immigrants and domestic workers in this State. As a Senator, I represent one of the most ethnically diverse districts in the state. I often proudly proclaim that my district — with the largest Pakistani community outside of Pakistan; the largest concentration of Haitians outside of Haiti; an even larger concentration of Caribbean nationals in the state and the largest orthodox Jewish community outside of Israel — looks like Brooklyn, looks like New York, and it looks like America.

The women of *The True Nanny Diaries* may be fictional but their stories send a sobering message that has stimulated my enthusiasm as an elected official. I hope it does the same for you.

Acknowledgments

I AM EXTREMELY GRATEFUL TO THE CREATOR, in all his glory, for my life and lessons. I give thanks to the divine messengers who open doors and clear my paths. I uplift my ancestors who have gone before. Ashe! Ashe! Ashe! This novel was never a solitary exercise. I am particularly grateful for my husband, Omidiran Khali Kwodwo Keyi-Ogunlade, for the constancy of his love and support. I thank him for his dedicated proofing and for believing in this project on the many days that I did not. I thank my daughter Kenya Nsoromma, who always lights my path. Special thanks to my parents David and Merlyn Jacob and Yolanda Jacob.

I am grateful to have met many extraordinary women on the playgrounds of New York City, particularly on the grounds of Columbia University, who shared their stories with me. This book would not exist without you. I am thankful for State Senator Kevin Parker of the New York Senate who has written a sterling introduction to this novel, and wholeheartedly supports the efforts to legally enshrine job protection for domestic workers in New York. Special thanks to Dr. Susan Fischer, who encouraged me to write this story.

On the technical side, I thank my judicious editor Marguerite Martindale of Wildmind Communications, whose monumental talents are all over this novel. Marguerite went beyond the editing call and transported me easily over that last high hill. I also thank my brilliant book designer, Michael L. Lawrence/MasTypography Studio, for his superb layout and, his patience. Blondie, I could always count on you, thanks for an awesome cover!

As for two powerful women in my life: my cousin-friend, Dr. Hazel Duncan and my sistah-friend Glenda Cadogan of Mauby Media, I absolutely appreciate your constant encouragement and support. Pure love and thanks to my relatives, Cynthia Jacob, Pastor Marilyn Ann Johnson, Clarissa Duncan, Gene Johnson, Garfield Duncan, Wynester Roberts and Anthony Celestine, and my friends Dr. Oseogun Awolabi, Dr. Delridge Hunter, Danella Abbey, Acklima Lopez, Fitz Moath, Michael Esdaille, and, of course, Leslie Dundas of Building By Faith Printing in Brooklyn. Pure love and thanks to Oloye Olakela Massetungi, Rev. Donna Faria, Rev. Pura Taylor, Rev. Andy Edwards and Geronimo Davidson, the spiritual mentors and teachers who propped me up in some way to make this novel a reality. Finally!

NANNY ON THE MARKET!!
She crawls on the floor! She dances!
She clowns! She wrestles! She makes faces!
My girls really adore her
but our needs have changed and
we want to find her a good home.

Amid sheaves of fading notices about long-filled jobs, long-lost cats, and "Stop the Iraq War" efforts, a pink sheet of paper printed with bright red ink, gleamed like a newly sewn patch on a raggedy old quilt. It was an ad titled, "Live-in Nanny Position."

Tear-away strips of the telephone number, which laced the bottom of the ad, hung untouched. I couldn't believe I had found this ad about a "Live-in Nanny Position" in Manhattan's Upper East Side, perhaps minutes after it had been posted. My luck was turning. A wisp of hope sparked. I had finally wedged my foot in a door early. Behind me, white women in their twenties, the type I usually worked for, sipped coffee as they discussed ways to help Third World Women.

I wasn't leaving nothing to chance. I would pull the ad down so no other babysitter would see it. I reached up. Then it hit me that the person who had posted the ad could be in the coffee shop watching me. I dropped my hand, and read:

Live-in Nanny Position
Our babysitter needs a home.
   She crawls on the floor!
She dances! She clowns! She wrestles!
   She makes faces!
My girls really adore her but our needs have changed
   and we want to pass her on to a good family.

It was a nanny, and not a nanny position, that was available. That ad should have been titled, "Live-in Nanny *Available,*" not "Live-in Nanny Position." Another wasted day spent scratching 'round for babysitting work in December, like hen scratch other chickens' shit for food. Misery descended in curtains of graduated shades of gray.

I wanted to call it a day, but that option did not take into account my looming homelessness. I would continue on to check job listings at the Y.M.C.A. and at that big church on the West Side. Later, before Christmas lights covered the city like a plague of fireflies, I would return to the basement room by the rasping boiler and go straight to sleep.

I tried to push 'way the gray haze around me with reassuring thoughts that something good going to happen to me soon. At the very least, I could count my blessings that I wasn't working for that person who had described the babysitter like a monkey on that pink paper.

She crawls on the floor! She dances! She be shuckin' and jivin' in mah kitchen a-l-l day long.

Thoughts of that ad inspired a l-o-n-g Caribbean woman suck-teeth that zigzagged inside my mouth, and screeched through my teeth, "Steeeeeeuuuuups."

Go back! Valdi girl, go back and read that ad on the pink paper again. You missed something important. Read it again!

I clapped my ears shut, but that only trapped the singsong, whining voice inside my head.

Valdi, you listen to me. I said, go back and read the ad again. Right now!

I had already put six blocks between me and the coffee shop when I finally turned around and headed back.

> **Live-in Nanny Position**
> *Our babysitter needs a home.*
> *She crawls on the floor!*
> *She dances! She clowns! She wrestles!*
> *She makes faces!*
> *My girls really adore her but our needs have changed*
> *and we want to pass her on to a good family.*

I buss out laughing. The ad had to be a big, fat joke posted by some activist protesting employer views of babysitters or something like that. It was the only explanation. No employer would describe a babysitter like that and post a phone number for everybody to see.

You missing something!

My eyes darted over the ad, focusing on the strips of numbers dangling neatly at the bottom. I remove a strip and examine it from the proximity of my palm.

Gyrl, this number don't ring a bell?

Suddenly, the piece of paper scorches my palm. I flick my hand and it drops, but the burning ent stop. Fire rips through the right side of my body like over proof muscle rub, sending sweat gushing through my pores. I want to vomit, I want to pee, my tongue get heavy and my whole body tremble. I grab hold of a garbage can that was below the bulletin board, and throw my mind back to hometown waters, Clifton Hill Beach, where I used to swim as a child. The burning stops, but not before a massive explosion in my right shoulder.

I didn't know when I grabbed the sheet of pink paper from the bulletin board, or when I left the coffee shop, or how I came to lose two hours lying prone on a park bench on E. 72nd Street, about seven blocks from the coffee shop. But when my brain clicked back to the present, the pink paper was crumpled in a ball in my hand, and my right shoulder blade was vibrating like a Shango drum was beating inside it. I spread open the pink paper and used my cell phone to dial the number. I did not expect anyone to answer. I did not want to leave a message. I just wanted to make that red phone on the green marble kitchen counter, above the room where I slept, ring. I wanted the sound of that ringing to send me catatonic with rage. Instead, the idea that this woman would equate my years of good service to herself and her daughters to the antics of a monkey make me crumble into a million pieces.

I picked up the pink paper again and dashed across Fifth Avenue, floating above the blaring horns, screeching tires and cussing drivers. I ran past the line-up at the bus stop, and entered Central Park on foot. Though the bus could cover the three miles to my three friends in a few minutes, I wanted to walk and run in the brisk breeze to collect the pieces of myself before I met the girls. The voice sang jingles in my head.

I got a monkey, a monkey. A monkey name Val. I got a monkey, a monkey name Val.

Even Ava would see the injustice that had been done to me.

THE STATUE OF FAMED Union General William Sherman Tecumseh was the central attraction of Grand Army Plaza, in central Manhattan. A smiling December day, after days of blinding snow, had pulled endless people to the area, blocking my direct view to the statue. I stepped on top a short concrete wall at the entrance to the Plaza, and looked over to the steps of the statue, where I expected my friends would be. I was specifically looking for Ava.

The brilliant sunshine blazed like a brazen shield between the statue and me. I smoothed the pink paper and used it as a visor, but I still couldn't identify the human forms on the statue's steps. For that matter, I could not see the huge gilded bronze figure of General Sherman or his fierce, rearing horse. Nike, the Athenian Goddess of Victory that leads the pair, seemed all alone on the granite pedestal. But Nike was not lonely as she rested in the arms of a golden sun.

The specter of the sun's rays, smothering Nike with kisses, took my breath away. I could finally see why American tourists flocked here, to see a horse, a soldier and a Goddess carved in the finality of stone. In the three years the girls and I had hung out in Grand Army Plaza, this was the first time I had ever been *soused* with emotion as I gazed at the statue. The usual value of General Sherman's statue, at least for us Caribbean babysitters in New York City, was as a shield against winter's quarreling winds, and a reliable signpost for arranging play dates, as in: "Meet me by Sherman."

A babysitter I didn't know pushed her stroller past me, "Valdi, oye! I hear you still looking for something to do. Gyrl, it hard out there, but I will keep my ears open. Go on, your friends by Sherman statue."

That a new babysitter on the circuit would have the details of my unemployment meant I was a ripe fruit on the nannyvine. She was talking to me like I now come in this town. And, as if I don't know that my friends would be by Sherman's horse's right flank, when we been *liming* there for a couple years! Even city workers on their lunch break knew Sherman's right side was ours. White folks from the neighborhood stayed across the courtyard under the oak tree. Other babysitters would stop and say "hello" to us, and then move on to their own spots deeper in the park. Even bitter winter afternoons would find the four of us there, though only long enough to ensure the children would say "yes" if their parents asked whether they had played in the goddamn snow that day.

I saw Ava. Not on the statue steps, but on the grass throwing a ball with girls. I called out. She waved stiffly and threw the ball in the opposite direction. She was on her so-called children-focused aspect of the afternoon. She was not to be disturbed. I wanted to sit her down immediately and rub the pink paper all over her know-it-all face and see her grapple for words to explain away this insult. There was time enough for that.

I walked to the steps leading to the statue. Madam Lucian and Monica were seated about a dozen steps high, on a long, wide platform. Monica was bouncing two babies on her knees. The one on her left knee was the one she was being paid to look after, the baby on her right knee was a tiny fraction of Madam Lucian's huge responsibility. As usual, Madam Lucian's face was welded to the blueprint for the fancy house she was constructing in St. Lucia.

At the base of the steps, the strollers my friends used were parked in a row. The front of Madam Lucian's three-part stroller monstrosity featured a reclining front seat for the baby. The middle of the contraption had a partially fenced, bucket seat for the oldest child, a disabled boy. The back was a cycling device for the six-year-old boy, which featured a bicycle seat mounted on a long iron pole; at its base was a footrest. The so-called stroller had been fashioned by Madam Lucian's boss who clearly imagined himself an inventor. He had proudly insisted that, if Madam Lucian let the six-year-old pedal as she pushed, the work of carting 150 pounds of children would feel like she on autopilot.

The disabled boy was asleep in his seat, with his head drooping at a disturbing angle. I took his baby brother's blanket from the front seat, rolled it into a wad and propped up his neck. In the three weeks since I last saw him, coarse hairs like wiry needles had punctured his upper lip, though his squat and babyish limbs belied his thirteen years.

Parked next to the contraption was the sleek, pink, jogging stroller that Monica's health nut employers had provided as a loud hint that she needed to drop some size. There was a three-foot gap, and then came the aerodynamic, gold-plated lord of the heap, double stroller that Ava used for the twins. My eyes wandered to the gap that would have accommodated my stroller if I was working. It was as though my friends were holding my place until I could find a job. The curtain of gray that had enshrouded me since the shit in the coffee shop suddenly evaporated. I attacked the stairs with vigor, running toward Madam Lucian and Monica, waving the pink paper for them to see.

"Valdi, ah wha dat?" Monica said.

Her tone was grainy, like she had answered the phone in her sleep. I resisted the urge to tell her that she sounded like she talking to a mister in the dark, which would have immediately taken the conversation to *bacchanal talk* before I had a chance to explain what the woman had done. Madam Lucian's head hadn't budged from the blueprint. I signaled to Monica to *dress rong*. She picked up the babies and stepped down a few stairs. I plopped down next to Madam Lucian, tumbling into her lap.

"Valdi, girl, I old. I old," she squawked.

"Gie me dat," I said, making a playful grab for the blueprint, but she nimbly hauled the plan behind her back.

"Not bad for an old, hard fowl, heh. You think I didn't see you? Heh."

Madam Lucian threw one hand over me, hugging me on her lap.

"Thanks for fixing the boy's head. Now what is on that paper you was waving?"

Monica returned to her seat, as I explained that I had gone into a coffee shop earlier that afternoon to check a bulletin board, only to discover that the woman had posted a notice about me. I did not have to explain who woman I was talking 'bout, as many Caribbean babysitters, in times of irritation (which was often), called their female employers dat behind their backs.

"Now I will read what the woman wrote about me on this pink paper," I told Madam Lucian and Monica.

I cleared my throat so I could recite with the inflections that the woman had intended.

"Live-in nanny position. Our babysitter needs a home. She cr-a-a-a-a-wls on the floor!"

"Valdi, may I see that?"

Ava had walked up the stairs and was standing right beside me. I started from the beginning for her benefit, but she grabbed the pink paper and began to read aloud, using a flat, nasal tone that drained all the condescending inflections from the piece. When she was finished, the others looked blank, but I posed my question anyway.

"All yuh don't think that the woman makes me sound like a monkey?"

Before Madam Lucian or Monica could say a word, Ava accused me of something incredible. She said I was being, get this, "fussy."

"Fussy?" I queried. "Fussy!?"

Miss Ava launched into such a vigorous defense of the woman that I only half-jokingly asked if they were in collusion. She pinched my arm hard. Ava could be mean like that. When I bawled out, she giggled, "See, Valdi? I keep telling you that your skin is too thin. That's why trivial things will always offend you."

"She should have titled this ad, 'Live-in Monkey Available,'" because this Valdi sound like one," I said, grabbing back my paper.

"Missy, she did *not* say monkey. Furthermore, she did not say Valdi, either. Your attitude is one of unpolluted ingratitude. May

I remind you that you would be homeless if the same person you disparagingly refer to as 'the woman' did not allow you to stay on in her house? It is babysitters like you that muddy the waters for everyone."

And so it went between us. Back and forth, another verse in the epic Ava-Valdi squabble, which would be postponed only when one of us left Grand Army Plaza in a huff. But I didn't want that, not today. It had been a while since I had been with the girls, and I wanted to set aside my troubles and just *lime.*

"Monica that voice you greeted me with sounded like you was whispering to a mister in the dark. Don't talk to me so. I am your friend, not your fella," I said.

Monica smiled wanly. Madam Lucian didn't even hear because she back with the house plans. Ava did not even acknowledge my attempt to *done the talk* about the pink paper. She poked Madam Lucian and asked her and Monica, "Do you agree with me or Valdi on this so-called monkey ad?"

She stared them down as if to say: *Dare you disagree with me, whose mouth holds a multi-syllabic prescription for every sore?*

The left side of Madam Lucian's mouth drooped, as she realized Ava expected an answer. When she asked to hold the paper, her voice had no music. She bowed over it for such a long time that Ava poked her again. Perhaps, Madam Lucian had hoped that the stillness she had imposed would inspire a new discussion, but we were dealing with Ava.

Madam Lucian's verdict sliced the silence. "Don't mind this paper, Valdi, sweetie, your boss heart is in the right place. She trying to help you find a work. It's just her way."

Tomcat Ava smiled.

"Madam Lucian, you would say that because you think everybody good. Even dem people you working for, who killing you with dem three children."

I focused on the words only when they tumbled out of my mouth, because to see their formation in my belly might send me bawling through the park at the injustice of it all.

"Madam Lucian, give me my paper, please." I tapped my palm. Her hand shook as she gave it back. I read the notice aloud, the way it should be read.

"Live-in Nanny Position. Our babysitter needs a home. She craaaaawls on the floor! She dances! She clooowns! She wrestles! She makes faces! My girls really adore her but our needs have changed and we want to *PASS HER ON* to a good family.

"Is me she talking 'bout here, and I have a right to my feelings even if nobody agree with me. It don't have to say, 'Live-in Nigger Available' for me to understand it's disrespect and racism."

Ava rolled her eyes and let out a series of clucks, disbelief caking her face.

"Valdi, you ... you ... you are not serious, right? You don't believe what you are saying, right?" She was so angry she was stuttering. "Monica, do you think that what is written here is racist?"

As Monica held Ava's gaze, a pink bubble blossomed between her lips, growing larger and larger until she pulled it in with a loud snap.

"What we ah do next Saturday night?" she queried.

It was a seemingly benign question, clearly delivered in the tone of don't dare pull me into *onno rass nonsense.* No smile dented the diagonal scar that divided Monica's face from nose to temple with a startling, miraculous skip over her right eye.

That afternoon, it was Ava who left Grand Army Plaza in a huff.

I WAGED MY CRUSADE ALONE, seizing ads from bulletin boards and flagging Internet postings. Meanwhile, the woman's phone would not stop ringing. Seems like everyone wanted to meet this monkey.

I called five hundred a week, even though my final salary before I was fired was three-fifty. I made sure to say this pay was for one child. The woman shadowed me anxiously whenever I took a call.

"This sounds like a great opportunity, dear," was her mantra as she passed me the phone.

I would cough crudely into the receiver, before answering sweetly, "Hello, this is Valdi." If the woman handed over the phone and walked away, I would say, "This is monkey." I was not working for anyone who would respond to an ad like that.

After every call, I told the woman, "Not the one."

"Don't settle, dear. You are part of the family. Stay as long as you want."

I knew that was a lie, long before I heard her whispering into the phone that I had her under siege in her own home. I didn't want to be in her house, but I would leave when I was good and ready. She was not getting a Hail Mary pass for upsetting my applecart on the cusp of winter with her "changed needs."

News of my firing was delivered one Friday night when she had unexpectedly come home early. She had stuck to me like a tick until I had scrubbed her house from top to bottom, erected a nine foot Christmas tree, and did the bath and bed routine with the girls. Then she invited me to sip hot chocolate as we discussed an "opportunity." As hailstones slammed against the window and thunder laughed in the sky, the woman said the girls' names had arrived at the top of some list for a prestige school. So, effective Monday, I had no job.

"But this is December. You better define what you mean by 'Monday,'" I said, knowing it was the one in three days, because that is how some of these people behave.

At least she had enough manners to blush. She said in lieu of notice she would give me three weeks pay and, if I agreed to move from the bedroom on the main floor to the room next to the boiler in the basement, I could stay on until I found a new position. She smiled like the matter had been settled with minimum discomfort. But, later, when she skipped down the stairs to show me the children's school uniforms, the *cut eye* I gave her made her evaporate up the stairs.

PILAR'S LEGACY

Two months after I first saw the ad, no one was calling, and I bare-ly had two pennies to rub together. The woman got blunt. "I need my basement," she said.

Around that time, Ava dropped by with what, considering my circumstances, should have been good news. It was about eight o'clock in the morning, and I was in bed trying to figure out how to tackle the day. It had been about a week since I had last gone out, in case the woman realized she could change the locks in my absence. I was also running out of ideas about finding full-time, well-paying work. People offered a day here and a day there. Enough of these could be patched together to make a week, but who want-ed to be zigzagging to a different apartment in Manhattan every day? Plus, I didn't have my own place to use as a base, so noth-ing else but full-time, live-in or live-out work would do.

Lying there, I got an idea to print business cards and give them to mothers in the park. I swung my legs to the ground and stood up. I heard rustling in the hall and my name being called in Ava's voice. Before I could react, my door was knocked on and pushed open in the same instant.

I saw only a flash of Ava's orange outfit before I dove back into the bed and pulled the blanket over my head. In my best moments, I felt like an unmade bed next to Ava. Having her find me with crusts of *yampee* around my eyes, and the room in total disarray, brought on that familiar, sinking feeling. Trust the woman to let Ava come downstairs without warning. I lay in silence. Ava had not said a discernible word since "Valdi." Instead, her disgust was conveyed in raspy breaths, tiny grunts and a few deep sighs. The sounds percolated through the weave of my blanket, coating me with shame.

My God, I knew Ava was thinking, *why is Valdi so bent on abusing her employer's generosity? Look at this room! She lives like a pig. She is a pig!*

"Valdi, come out from under that blanket." She said this very, very softly, as if she was using someone else's voice.

I wet my finger under my tongue and used the spit to remove the crusts of mucus from the corners of my eyes. I tongued the corners of my mouth to erase dry drool. Then I eased my hands around the bed until my fingers touched the satin of my headscarf. I remained under the blanket as I tied the scarf over my head to envelop my tussled hair weave. Finally, I pulled the blanket from my face and flinched. Ava was leaning over me, with her lips as pinched as a closed purse.

"Valdi, who dropped a bomb in here?"

"Yeah, like that line is so original. Must you hover over me like that?"

She turned away furiously then strutted from the headboard to footboard, swinging her crocodile skin briefcase. She spun around and repeated the walk, her high-heeled boots showing off her six-foot model's figure to perfection. She pelted her hips — but daintily — flaunting her Coca Cola bottle shape. Not the modern-day plastic coke bottle that shape like a tub, but like the old-time glass bottle from back home, which was pinched in the middle and then flared dramatically like my mother's hips. Long time when I walked with mother, men and women alike would whisper, "Petra shape like Coco-Cola bottle even after she done make two *chirren,* lawd." Then they fanned themselves vigorously, because lust and jealously both provoked flashes of heat.

Ava would not stop. 'Round and 'round she went, up and down. She was like a *frizzle fowl* getting ready to lay eggs.

In a rush of anger, I flung off the covers and pulled myself up. I leaned over and moved a pile of clothes from the bedside chair to the bed. "Sit!"

She looked at the chair, her gaze fixing on a *peeny,* little spot of nothing. She leaned towards me, gingerly selecting a large towel from the pile. She folded it several ways and placed it on the supposedly offending area. Then she took off her own silk scarf that she doubled and spread on the towel.

"Doan get no pressure, but orange clothes *dutty* quick," she said.

Ava sat, without removing her coat, balancing her briefcase between her knees. The fact that this sentence was delivered in Guyanese patois, and featured a pedestrian word like "dutty," made me very anxious. Ava never talked slang unless she was in the middle of wukkin' you over.

"You just think that your bottom better than everybody else own," I said. She didn't say anything.

"So why you didn't say you were coming? Ah woulda fix something for you to eat. Let me go upstairs to the kitchen," I said, wiggling my toes as though I intended to get up.

"That's not necessary, Valdi. I am calling on you with purpose, not pleasure. Meeting you like this makes my news more pertinent. Valdi, gyrl, I don't know what to think. I don't know what to say. What the dickens is going on with you?"

Suddenly, I was amused. It was nice having Ava not knowing what to think let alone what to say. The nastiness of the room was confusing to her because she had diagnosed me as being "excessively and obsessively neat." She had whined to Madam Lucian and Monica that I used too much sanitizing gel. As though she was the one paying for it. Since then, I hid behind the washroom wall in the park whenever I wanted to cleanse my hands. To have rendered Ava speechless almost made me regret fingering out the yampee crust from my eyes.

"Pilar's boss is seeking a nanny."

Once again, Ava had vacuumed me into the darkness of dumb wonderment, where I waited for a punch line, twinkling eyes, any indication that she was joking. Ava's sober countenance, as she met my gaze, reflected her astounding capacity for sweeping rich people's shit under the Persian.

"Ava, didn't Pilar's boss say she would not hire no immigrant to watch her child?"

"Valdi, as you know, I do not get entangled in whispering campaigns, gossip, malicious chitter, neither chatter. I am also not here for *ole talk*. I came to present you with an opportunity to have first dibs at an excellent situation."

I wanted to know more about this development in the Pilar saga, but getting talk from Ava was harder than digging food from a rotten molar. She took pride in demonstrating how much she hated other people's business.

"Ava, if you want me to take the job, at the very least you must say how it became yours to give."

She offered stony silence, until I leaned over and began troubling the cuticle in my big toe.

"Madam Lucian, Monica and I were sitting by General Sherman Tecumseh's statue as usual, when Chloë left the oak tree, walked across the plaza and up the stairs toward us. She was extremely warm in her greeting, and I responded likewise. Madam

Lucian and Monica briefly said 'hello' before leaving to take the children to the bathroom. Chloë sat next to me and said that she had been sitting under the oak admiring my relationship with the children. She asked if I would consider changing families. Naturally, I told her that I am blissfully happy with my family."

"Of course, blissfully happy." I interjected sarcastically.

Ava continued as if I hadn't spoken. "The babies cooed and showered me with kisses. Chloë smiled and said, 'I have a baby, too. Please guide me to the perfect babysitter to be part of our family.'"

"And is here you park your umbrella, Mary Poppins? Avaaaah, come on, I am looking for a work not a family."

"She pays well and you need a new situation."

I grabbed a fork from the nightstand and started to dig out the cuticle. She put her hands over her eyes.

"Is that yours or does it belong to your employer?" she said, biting disgust dripping like pepper sauce from her words.

"The fork is mine, but the cuticle is theirs," I said, dropping the fork in the garbage.

"Valdi, you have too much time on your hands. Just today we were saying that you need a job. Madam Lucian said you can take her job when she departs for St. Lucia, but that's a long time."

"Madam Lucian must be crazy. Nobody wants that job." We both laughed.

"Anyway, you don't need Madam Lucian's job. This is yours for the taking. From where I stand, you don't have a choice."

"I choosing to stay black and die, girl; there's always that."

"You just might die in here," Ava said, wrinkling up her nose like she was talking to a pebble of goat shit. According to the old people proverb, *It's the change from the dollar that makes the noise,* so I let Ava's insult pass.

"I gave your number to Chloë. I'll give you hers as well. Call her. Valdi, it is urgent that you leave this home. You are not welcome here."

"Steeeeups."

"Please stop that juvenile hissing. Be reasonable; the job is a live-out situation, and there is an apartment I could get for you in Brooklyn on Midwood Avenue."

"I don't do Brooklyn."

"Because you have never had a live-out job. The apartment is five blocks from Utica Avenue, which is the last stop on the No. 4 train. It would take fifty minutes to arrive at Chloë's place on E. 67th Street. Valdi, you don't want to be able to go home on evenings? Turn the keys to your own place? Please, gyrl, take this job before you sink further into depression."

"Who say I depressed, eh? You always on that psycho crap." I snapped my fingers and pointed Ava to the door. She was only a sophomore in college, but thought she knew already how to diagnose everybody.

"Depression is nothing to be ashamed about."

"You back right up. Don't even try to psyche me out. I am not a case in your textbook."

"Valdi, I have been observing you for weeks and doing the research. I have discussed you with professors. I wrote a midterm paper based on you. You are displaying classic symptoms of SIGECAPS."

"SIGECAPS?"

A thunderous crack, trailed by a succession of cackling sounds, shot from behind me. I spun sharply to check it out only to realize it was my own laughter. I casually fluffed the pillows before turning back to Ava.

"SIGECAPS? SIGECAPS? Ava, whaddat? The name of your big butt?"

Ava's face froze, then crumbled. She rose painfully; her hands clasped around her belly as though my words had caused physical pain. Ava hated the jut of her bottom. Like a fool, I brought the topic back to me.

"Come, come, girl, that's why you studying so hard at college, to come here talking foolishness about SIGECAPS?"

Immediately, she bent and pulled out a thick textbook from her briefcase, sat back down and opened it on her lap. She put on her tortoise-shell glasses and peered at me like I was a delinquent student.

"SIGECAPS, a mnemonic device used to diagnose depression, was invented by Gross," she informed me. She then launched into a description of what mnemonic means like she alone went to school.

"'S' is for an increase or decrease in sleep. 'I' is for lost interest in pleasurable activities, like intimacy. 'G' is for feelings of guilt. 'E' is for lack of energy. 'C' is for problems with concentration. 'A' is for appetite increase or decrease. 'P' is for psychomotor agitation. 'S' is for idealizing suicide and hallucinations. Valdi, you have at least six of these symptoms."

Ava placed the open book on the chair and started cat walking again. She would make a so-called point beginning with "Valdi" and walk to the foot of the bed. She would make another supposed point that also began with "Valdi," and then walk back to the head of the bed.

"Valdi, you don't have the desire to clean this mess.

"Valdi, you have not ventured from this basement for weeks.

"Valdi, you have not mentioned an intimate partner in a while.

"Valdi, why is your right shoulder palpitating like that?

"Valdi, you are unable to concentrate on finding a job.

"Valdi, you are edgy and unpleasant.

"Valdi, you have gained at least thirty pounds.

"Valdi, I'm sure you are hearing voices, seeing things."

I couldn't say nothing. It was like being in front a jury hearing "guilty," "guilty," "guilty." I coughed to cover up my search for a good comeback. When all I could manage was a sarcastic, "Anything else?"

"I'm glad you asked. The only symptom that is not identifiable from observation is whether you have feelings of worthlessness, hopelessness or even suicidal thoughts. Valdi, do you hallucinate? Do you think that you are you better off dead?"

Ava suddenly leaned over me on the bed. I had to slide down to get out her way. She looked like she was about to shove a stethoscope up my ass. It occurred to me that she was more concerned with her diagnosis being correct than the possibility that I might want to out my lights.

"Ava, the reason I don't go nowhere is because I have no money to go there with. I purposely leave the room this way to irritate the woman upstairs."

A low steeeeups accidentally emerged from Ava's mouth. "Pardon me. Excuses, Valdi," she said. "One last question."

"What?"

"When was the last time you participated in an intimate encounter?" She was blushing, her words barely discernable, like it was a bloody virgin talking.

"You mean sex?"

She nodded.

"With or without someone?" I winked.

She dropped that talk. People like Ava do not masturbate.

"The circles under your eyes mean no sleep."

"Noise upstairs."

"The thirty pounds?"

"Ten."

"What about your right-shoulder spasms?"

"Check your left eye."

"Hallucinations, feelings of guilt, worthlessness or suicidal thoughts?"

"Never said I have that."

"Do you?"

"Ava, I have one problem. I need a job."

"Now that is the reason I came. Call Pilar's boss, Valdi."

"I do not want to."

"Look," her voice rose sharply, but she checked it. "At least, take it until something else comes up. You can't stay here without prospects just borrowing money."

It's always a bad idea to let people know your business. Ava spoke with authority because, the last time she dropped by, she pressed a hundred dollar bill in my palm when she realized I had no food.

"Look, I am not trying to make you feel bad. I'm saying that, if I were in your situation, I would take this job. Look, the money is certain. Chloë owns the largest communications and event planning firm in the country."

Ava picked up her briefcase and packed up the book.

"Write down the number, then at least you'll have it."

I didn't disturb a muscle even when she pick up my diary from the nightstand, shift the torn cover and scribble inside. Her parting shot was delivered as a plea.

"The number is on the first page. Things are not the same at the statue without you. If you take this position, you will remain part of the Upper East Side circle. Suppose you get a job on the West Side that forces you to mingle with those low-class babysitters over there? Please think about it, Valdi."

Ava's parting words, minus the bullshit about low-class babysitters, touched me. As disgusting as she could be, seventeen years of friendship is seventeen years of friendship.

We met back in '87, in the laundry room of an apartment complex called The Stowers on 79th. As the only two Caribbean domestic workers in the building, Ava and I became friends though, at seventeen, she was almost ten years younger than me. Back then, I was a maid in uniform, while Ava served mostly as a com-

panion for a sixteen-year-old white girl whose older husband travelled continuously. I didn't last six months on my job but, all this
time, Ava was still in the same job because her employers make
six children, moved to a fancy townhouse, and showered her with
money. I had held about a dozen jobs to Ava's one, but stayed on
the Upper East Side so we could do play dates and lime.

It wasn't until much later that we started liming with Madam
Lucian and Monica. Monica always knew where to find a good party in Brooklyn. Sometimes, she and I would go out on Saturday
nights and, as daybreak signaled Sunday, we would take a taxi to
Madam Lucian's apartment. Madam Lucian would have a rich mixture of salt fish, tomatoes, onions, pepper and olive oil, and spongy,
saffron buns waiting for us. She would faithfully head out to sev-
en o'clock mass and, when she returned, she would cook *Sunday
food.* Ava usually joined us after service at her evangelical
church in Manhattan, and we passed many Sundays together by
Madam Lucian's like this.

Holidays were also a time to be together: Thanksgiving and New
Year's Day at Madam Lucian's, Christmas at Ava's, while Monica
was the base for West Indian Day Parade *bacchanal.* We got to
know each other's relatives too: Monica's Tanty Vee, a Long Island
babysitter, and Madam Lucian's little brother, Boyo, who was her
man-of-business in St. Lucia. We also use to lime by Uncle Ram,
Ava's great-uncle, until he married Monica to help fix her papers
and got weird. That Monica was to become a naturalized American because of Uncle Ram really pissed me off, because I had
known him long before her.

Though I had pegged him as a good candidate for a Green-Card
marriage, I was waiting for him to volunteer to do it. The very first
day that Monica set foot in Uncle Ram's house, she told him that
she didn't see nothing looking like a wife among his pictures on
the mantel; she didn't see no woman clinging to him in the par-

ty; and, since he worked for the Department of Prisons, he must have his immigrant papers straight. In short, she was proposing a Green-Card marriage so she could be straight in America, too. Uncle Ram said he would do anything to help someone get settled in America, especially a woman with children like Monica. But, first, he marched her to the beauty parlor over ample objections of, "*rass,* no!" to get her a decent weave and trim her nail extensions. He also carried her to a boutique and bought her some decent clothes.

On the wedding day, Uncle Ram's yard looked like a set for a shoot for *Bridal Magazine.* Silver and white organza snaked through the wrought iron fence. A glass-top table, sprinkled with blue and silver rose petals, featured a six-tier, black rum cake topped with a windmill that churned water through a glass tunnel. Numerous electrical wires fed cameras that would record the day for immigration interrogators.

Monica had played Mrs. Bride to the hilt, flashing the big diamond that she had bought herself. Monica nearly dragged Uncle Ram's tongue out his mouth during the cake sticking, as workers from his job cheered lustily and knocked lead crystal glasses with sterling silver forks, while babysitters shook their heads knowingly. The deep-mouth kiss made Ava very nervous about this Green-Card marriage between Monica and her Uncle Ram, which was not supposed to have sexual perks. Ava was very stiff at the wedding reception that night. Monica tried to reassure Ava that it was strictly business as the four of us trudged up the steps to Madam Lucian's apartment at one o'clock in the morning after the wedding was over.

"Ava, wan, okay, two little business kiss between your uncle and me and you worried. See here, I still ah wear my wedding gown and I'm 'ere with the three of *onno,* when I should be 'ug up with my 'usband."

Ava dropped on the stairs and laughed till she was weak. Re-membering moments like these — joking around for the rest of the day with Ava and me still in our bridesmaid dresses, Madam Lu-cian in her mother-of-the-bride frock, and Monica in her corset and taffeta slip — made Ava's warning, that I might get a job on the West Side that would separate us, resound long after she had left.

We would part ways soon enough without that. Ava would grad-uate and begin her professional career. Uncle Ram promised to get Monica a job with the Department of Prisons after she got her Green Card and received her high school certificate. By then, Madam Lucian would surely be planting garden and sunning on her verandah in St. Lucia.

FOR A LONG TIME AFTER Ava had steered her strapped down back-side out the door, I wondered if I should consider Pilar's old job. Her visit had sapped the energy I was going to put into getting the business cards. I put the pillow over my head. Sleep had been al-most two days in coming and my body succumbed gratefully. Less than twenty minutes into my slumber, the woman and children came home and cut my sleep short. For nearly an hour, I sat lis-tening to the commotion from the basement steps.

The girls were begging for a dog like the one they had seen in an adoption van on the street. The mother was refusing, but one could only get so far with that damn magazine mothering. My right shoulder suddenly felt like it was stomping in its socket when the woman succumbed and promised to get them a dog — any dog that would make them shut up — the very next day. This could have been a ploy on her part, figuring they would forget about the dog by morning. But, I couldn't take the chance.

I run back to the room and found Pilar's boss' number in my diary. I siddown at the edge of the bed, and had dialed no further than the area code when I became aware that Pilar lay on the bed next to me, her lower body mangled like she just get pull from under that mail truck.

Papaa, yo! I spring from that bed and drop the phone. I run to the door and pull it; it wouldn't open. Pilar sat up and look at me with mournful eyes. Her face look old. Not the good-looking old that come when you live good and nearly done live, but the kind of hardening that come when you drag up every single morning to face the grind. Her hands clasped dem wooden building blocks that give white children soaring dreams, and I feel like somebody push me inside Richard Wright's poem, *Between the World and Me,* 'cause a sea of white folks appeared and set Pilar ablaze right there on the blasted bed.

I jumped out the *friggin'* hallucination.

Why Pilar pick me to haunt, when I had never said a word to her in life, was a mystery. When I first hear that a babysitter named Pilar, who frequented Grand Army Plaza, had been flattened by a mail truck, I couldn't even separate her from the body of Hispanic women going about their daily business. And I was not alone. None of the Caribbean babysitters could recall Pilar's specific face until Monica show us a Spanish language newspaper that carried a photo.

From what we hear, Pilar just up and decide to buy boots like her employer had purchased for a couple thousand dollars. For months, Pilar didn't send a single cent home, prompting her brother to travel through an underground tunnel from Tijuana to America.

"¿Estás loca, mujer? Watchoo especk you seben cheeeldren to eeeet?"

Pilar parted with the money in her wallet, but held fast to the dream. She walked to save bus fare. She took a weekend work seeing about an elderly man. One September day, when leaves were ripening, and cool breezes chiseled holes in the summer heat, Pilar had saved enough. She pushed the boy through Central Park to Madison Avenue to buy those boots.

The next day, Pilar went back to the store to return the boots. As she crossed Madison Avenue, she stepped into the path of a U.S. mail truck. For days, the nannyvine rippled with talk of her death. Venom was directed at Chloë, her employer, who was said to have demanded that Pilar choose between her job and the boots. Now, Ava wanted me to work for this same Chloë and reinvent myself inside the urn with Pilar's ashes!

I jammed the bed against the bedroom door, not knowing if to be more terrified of a dog coming upstairs or Pilar's returning downstairs. As day turned into night, and night turned into day, I stared out the window. I stared behind me.

Sleep finally knocked about 9:00 a.m., only to be murdered by a barking dog.

A WOMAN OPENED Pilar's boss' door as I raised my hand to ring the bell. Then she stepped up to me in the hall, locking her close-set eyes with mine. I figured she was about five-feet-five, like me. But when I averted my gaze to break the stare, I noticed her three-inch heels. She was still staring when our eyes met again.

"Good morning, I am here to see Chloë."

She stepped back into the apartment, and clipped-clipped across the foyer, waving me in. I tried to walk alongside, rather than behind her, because all she wore was a silk slip that didn't even pretend to hide the tiny piece of lace that was supposedly her panty.

She went straight to the nursery, which meant I would know whether the job was mine before the interview was over. She was the "cut-to-the-chase" type, and was not likely to skewer me with questions and repeat interviews. The baby in question was toddling around in a playpen in the same room. Any day now, he would make his toys into a mountain and attempt to stand on them and pull himself out. He was about a year old, so I would have about a year's peace before he would start mouthing off and giving grief.

"Hi, hi," he said looking at me and holding up his hands.

I started toward him, but Chloë pointed to a narrow cane loveseat and instructed me to sit. She sat on the loveseat, too, leaving very little space between us.

"What do you know about Pilar?"

I gripped my seat as my mind fought images of a burning Pilar. My brain raced through a series of possible answers: *(a) Who's Pilar? (b) Pilar who? (c) I don't know anything about, ah, um, who did you say? (d) What the hell does Pilar have to do with me?*

With a skip of only two beats, I settled on, *(e) None of the above.*

"We were not friends."

"I never said you were. I surmise, from your reference to Pilar in the past tense, that you know she's dead. I will sum up that event in one sentence. At least she didn't get my baby killed when she cavorted in front that mail truck. How could she miss a mail truck?"

That was two sentences.

The space between us tightened, as she raised one leg and sank her heel into the chair cushion. She turned her face to me.

"The day I saw her in my home wearing those boots, I said, 'Pilar, how can I trust you if you want to be me?'"

I nodded my head, as if I agreed that Pilar had no damn right to use money she worked for to buy what the hell she pleased.

I tried to figure out the woman's age. Was she twenty-five looking like thirty-five, or forty-five looking like thirty-five?

"Pilar was such a nincompoop," she said. "Look, I didn't mind giving her something outrageously expensive, and you will find that I am very generous. Fuck, I would have given her my own boots if she had asked, but for her to buy them herself … no fucking way. She could have murdered me; worn my panties. I have heard horror stories about nannies, but I hope you're not like that."

She waited for confirmation that, even if I were presumptuous enough to have ambition, it did not extend to wearing her panties.

I wanted to joke about my preference for nondescript drawers that cover my whole business but it didn't seem like a good idea. She sank into a deep silence. She wanted me to say that it was not her fault that Pilar's seven children were starving in Tijuana.

So, I clucked, "Tsk, tsk, tsk. Pilar, Pilar, Pilar. Why?"

It was not enough.

"Pilar brought this upon herself," I said firmly.

I had the job: four hundred and eighty dollars a week cash, plus a metro-card. Light cooking was required, and seeing about the baby boy who I was finally allowed to meet. He obligingly put his little chubby arms around my neck and found a spot on my breast. The woman was impressed.

I told her that my most recent job had been live-in, and that I had not yet found an apartment. She said I could move in temporarily. In fact, I should stay and get to know the baby, while she went out.

I called Ava to tell her I got the job. She gloated. I told her about the dog at my old job. She said she would make arrangements to fetch my things. I asked her to make an appointment for me to check out the apartment on Midwood Avenue. The next day, she called to say that she had paid the security and the first month rent as a gift. She also had "great news." The apartment was fully furnished. To her, it didn't matter that I had not seen the place, which turned out to be eleven steps under the earth, comprising three mouldy rooms with one two-by-one window in a wide hallway that Ava kept calling the "living room." There was barely any room to walk around the huge, casket-like, four-poster bed, with musty, crinkled satin drapery.

I felt a rising hatred for that bitch. She would not live in a place like that, so why was it good enough for me?

After Ava left, having deposited my things, I sat on a yellow, spotted, leather couch in the living room. Gradually, I inched myself off. The clammy, fuzzy surface had stuck to my butt like it was made from a frog's skin. I sat on a chair in the kitchen, with my head in my palms, and didn't move for a long time.

Considering the desperation that had forced me into Chloë's employ, it was shocking how painlessly three years had elapsed. I even remained in the same apartment Ava had arranged. I tried to make the apartment as homey as possible. I asked the landlord, an old Grenadian schoolmistress, to take her furniture out the basement. When she refused, I removed the satin canopy, and replaced it with blue organza. I encased the frog-skin, leather couch in a yellowish canvas, and tried to forget what was stewing underneath. Hundreds of sticks of incense and boiled potpourri gradually overpowered the mold. If the apartment could be pushed above the earth, it would have been *so-so,* at least, for someone who couldn't have an apartment in her name.

As for the work, Pilar never haunted me again, and her old boss proved no better or worse than the rest. In all the time I worked there, we had only one disagreement. Back when the boy was two, she had heard him humming the theme song from a soap opera. She didn't make a fuss. She just said that though island people like soaps, she wanted me to put her son down for a nap first. I just dropped the whole soap opera thing, which was a stupid pastime I had picked up from Monica. When the boy started half-day school, Chloë fired the housekeeper and gave me the housework, rather than reduce my hours. It was the longest I had ever worked for any employer in America.

Everyday at 8:00 a.m., I would pick up the boy and drop him off at the nursery school for his environmental awareness class. I would return to the house to clean, sleep, read or watch TV. At one, Ava and I would meet at the school where we picked up the children. Then we would take the bus over to the statue to meet Madam Lucian and Monica.

So, up to the moment I met Delia, I was rocking in the bosom of complacency 'cause things weren't bad. And, until such time as some damn thing happened, it just was what it was.

Most importantly, I was grateful to be working, and glad the rhythm was predictable on this work. On Monday and Tuesday I worked with the boy on learning when to say "thank you," "please" and "excuse me." By Wednesday morning he had stopped expelling gas around folks and giggling uproariously. Come Thursday, he would flush the toilet after use. By Friday, my sweetheart's long goodbye made me miss the 6:15 p.m. train.

The following Monday, I had to start the manners thing all over again, because the father allowed him to run amok on the weekends. When he launched his grand experiments, it was usually with me, or so the father would have me believe. He capsized the little aquarium and looked on as Focus, the fish, flapped his dying gills. He slammed his feces on the ceiling to see if "gravity works on shit." He stepped from the window sill on to the white enamel strip on the stove, in his new-brand shoes, between a pan of frying chicken strips and boiling noodles, simply because he could.

These antics, with jail written all over them, kept me busy as he grew. On his bad days, he robbed me of a single adult thought in a whole damn day. It was enough to make an elephant weep. I would tell him, "Boy, if I collected just one black cent every time you say 'Valdi,' your mother wouldn't ever have to pay me."

But, still, my heart grew soft for him, more than for any other child I had taken care of. He could crawl inside your heart, using dem large brown eyes, with a smile that made you feel that you really mattered. That was on his good days.

I feared his disdain for the middle way. With him, it was either vinegar or honey.

The day that fate thrust Delia and me together, after seventeen years, that boy was rocking vinegar.

The dollar-van driver who Madam Lucian paid monthly to purchase a fifty-pound sack of flour and tote it to her second-floor apartment had left it, instead, at the restaurant on the ground floor. Mrs. Shu, the restaurant proprietor, mentioned this in between unsolicited mutterings about why I was having so much trouble turning the lock in the gray, metal door that led to Madam Lucian's apartment upstairs. She said I should sit in the restaurant and eat wanton soup and, when her son, Tian, came home from college, he would take the flour up.

"How is Tian doing in school?" I asked.

"Every night Tian read big books from college. No help with cook food," she beamed.

Mrs. Shu never missed an opportunity to say "Tian" and "college" in the same sentence.

"You sit with me?"

"Not today, Mrs. Shu. I'll take the flour upstairs, myself. I have a lot to do."

"You bake by yourself?" she asked, perplexed.

"The others will be here later, but I want to leave early tonight. I have big party tomorrow," I said, shaking the pantsuit in the dry-cleaning plastic bag that I held over my shoulder.

"I'm going to start the baking before my friends come."

"No soup?"

"No soup, Mrs. Shu. The flour, please."

I followed her into the restaurant, where she showed me the sack of flour sitting under a dining room table. Mrs. Shu held my dry cleaning, as I bent over to pull the flour from under the table. After her admonitions that I bend my knees, I stooped and bear-hugged the sack, and hobbled into a standing position. She suggested that I return for the dry cleaning after I had taken the flour up to Madam Lucian's, but I didn't want my pantsuit smelling like fried meat. I overrode her objections by insisting that she drape the garment bag on top the flour sack, and hook the wire hanger to the shoulder strap of my handbag.

Mrs. Shu followed me to the gray door, fished the bunch of keys from my coat, and unlocked the door with one turn. She blocked the entrance to the stairway, while she leisurely repositioned the dry cleaning to indicate it had already begun to slip off the sack. Mrs. Shu then tucked the keys in a fold in the garment bag and slammed the door behind me.

I cussed out the dollar-van driver twenty-three times, each time I had both feet on the same step and was gearing up to tackle one more. The sack of flour was no joke. I had to step first with my left foot, shove the full weight of the flour on to that thigh, and then heave up my right foot. By the time I arrived at the top, muscles in my back and the rear of my thighs were scraps of smoldering wood.

Halfway down the hall, both the keys and the dry cleaning bag fell, and my next step landed on something soft. I spared that not a thought. My focus was purely on Madam Lucian's red door, which, of course, would be located at the end of the hall. Plus, I figured the pantsuit was safe inside the plastic sheath.

Praps! I dropped the flour in front Madam Lucian's door. Mercifully, it did not burst open. I stretched and flexed all the way back to pick up my newly dry-cleaned pantsuit. The pressure from my foot had torn the plastic bag over it, leaving a perfect, half-sneaker print tattooed on the pants. Little did I know that it was merely a sign of things to come.

WE NEVER RUSHED ANYTHING when we made bread by Madam Lucian. She said the *oomph* that surrounds dough makers determines the final outcome of the bread. That's why I didn't go around by her during the dark days of my unemployment; I had carried bad oomph. The one day I went around to assist, the bread emerged from the oven resembling an old-time baking stone.

For the sake of the bread, I wanted to forget how pissed I was about bringing the flour up the stairs, getting the stain on my clothes, and being by Madam Lucian at all, when I could be home getting ready for the big day. I sat at Madam Lucian's kitchen table on "my chair." Each of the four chairs had evolved into Valdi's chair, Monica's chair, Ava's chair and Madam Lucian's chair. And whether we were working or liming, we always sat on the same seats: Ava facing the short wall, me facing Ava with my back to the fridge, Madam Lucian facing the long wall, and Monica facing Madam Lucian with her back to the kitchen counter.

At first, Madam Lucian had refused to allow me to go to her place and start the prep before she arrived. I told her that if I could not go to her house early and leave early, I wouldn't be able to help out. Ava said to count her out 'cause she had to study for midterms. Monica was useless, as she had been sniffling all day. That's when Madam Lucian handed me the keys, even though I was begging her in my mind for this one Friday night free. Not that our help was critical to her operation, as Madam Lucian had single-handedly baked and sold bread from her apartment for years before she met any of us — even Monica. She was more spoiled by having company than the actual help the company provided. I got a long lecture about the actual list of things I could do, and a much longer list of things I could not touch. The *siboa* she had left hanging over the radiator to dry was a big no-no. She had also warned me to take my time with the preparations.

"Do not put no hurry-hurry energy into my bread."

I anchored my elbows like an upside down "v," dropped my chin between my palms, and inhaled the lavender scent from the plant that Madam Lucian kept on the kitchen table. We teased her that lavender was her drug of choice. In the living room, its light floral scent exuded from satin satchels tucked under couch cushions. In the bathroom, the scent came from decorative purple soaps and tiny oil spots on the hand towels. In the kitchen, chemical lavender exploded from the freshly washed floor and the dried blue blossoms resting on the radiator cover. Madam Lucian was herself a walking lavender blossom, because she put a few drops in the clothes dryer, and would top that up with English lavender body mist after every shower.

But I always enjoyed her lavender most by breathing over the blossoms of the plant. The smell sent my mind wandering along the edges of memories, half-forgotten, before settling for the present and immediate. Like being in my own apartment preparing for the big day ahead, wrapping my hair, and slathering warm mud on my face. Then, most delicious of all, I imagined associating with the literati who were sure to be at the gala.

I wished I could go home to look for the specific shoes to match the pantsuit. Back in the day, I never bought an outfit without shoes to match. I wondered if, and how, the suit would fit. It would be my first attempt in years to wear a size nine. I had fetched the suit from an old chest after my boss asked why I always wore such "huge, ill-fitting garments."

She was the one who suggested I was probably a size nine under my "unsightly, floral tent." She wondered aloud what shape size nine I was.

"Are you the pear or hour-glass? I'm the wedge," she said. "All boobs, slight and tight," she offered, as she stepped into the boy's bedroom, with a peeny lacy top over her breasts.

Just the other day I had reminded her that Cole was five, and she must stop parading half-naked 'round the place. She said that I might want to examine why I was ashamed of my body. She said that, in all the years that I had worked for her, she had never once seen me in any state of undress. As if that was a job requirement!

I always step from the bathtub into my towel. I slip on my panties under the towel, and wiggle my bra over the towel. My shirt goes on before the towel comes off, and my pants go on before I step out the bathroom door. Maybe that comes from years spent living by people. It was just my way, like unwarranted exhibitionism was hers. She had me curious, though, about what shape size nine I might be. If, indeed, I was a size nine, it would mean that I had maintained the same size I had been when I stepped off the BWIA flight from Trinidad nineteen years ago. I would try on the suit before Madam Lucian arrived and, if it looked good enough, ask her to clean the stain.

Thoughts of Madam Lucian and a simultaneous crash of pots in Mrs. Shu's kitchen below stirred me into action. I washed my hands as thoroughly as if Madam Lucian were looking. I walked into the pantry to collect familiar things: the crock pot of Madam Lucian's homemade yeast, the wooden sieve to sift the flour, the purification system to filter water for the dough. From a white cloth, I extracted the bamboo kneading board, whose circular groves still gleamed from the poppy-seed, oil massage Madam Lucian gave it after each use.

There was a familiar and comforting rhythm to the whole process. The thought that I wouldn't be there when matchless whiffs of baking bread conquered the fumes from Mrs. Shu's kitchen made me feel sad.

Madam Lucian arrived late that night. Her people had kept her late, without pay, again. By the time she arrived, somewhere around nine, I had already sifted the pre-sifted flour twice. If Madam Lucian saw even a tiny clump, the flour would have to be sifted a third time. About ten minutes later, Monica arrived. She always went home to shower before she came to Madam Lucian's, ostensibly, "to wash off the work week." At least that's what she said. It was not lost on us that she always arrived in full make-up, perfume and fitted clothes to tantalize Madam Lucian's, mostly male clientèle. Couple minutes later, Ava came. She said she had not been able to focus on her studies, so she decided to come after all.

Madam Lucian washed her hands then tilted the bowl of sifted flour from side to side, nodding approvingly. She called me over from the kitchen counter where I had been filtering water for dough.

"You learn well, chile," she said.

The warm smile on her lips suddenly contracted and zipped, when she realized the siboa she had left in the wooden colander had been capsized into a bowl. Ava frowned. Monica looked on with open admiration that I had dared trouble Madam Lucian's *Garifuna* business. Madam Lucian would make the siboa into areba, a crispy, flat cassava cake that was popular with the men who hung out on Fridays at the Garifuna social club. I didn't get why she was upset; the siboa was sitting in the very bowl she always meant when she said, "Bring me the areba bowl."

"If you had to do something that I told you not to do, you should have tried to fry the fish, not play in my siboa," she sniffed.

It's only friggin' dry cassava. You taking people for granted. It's not like you pay for this help. There are a lot of other things I should be doing tonight.

Though this was only whispered in my mind, it did not stop shame from crawling over my thoughts.

My apology was heartfelt when I told Madam Lucian, "I'm sorry for troubling the siboa."

Madam Lucian's criticism had brought back my frustration about being there. She took her customary shower before tackling the baking. When she finally returned to the kitchen — dressed, as usual, in white, her long, silvery, tresses secured in a net — she moved like a snail. It didn't help that Monica didn't plan to help. She sat in the living room, inhaling over a bowl of steaming eucalyptus leaves and lavender flowers. Her moans of, "lawdy, lawdy, lawdy" pissed me off. The water meandering through the filter pissed me off. In fact, everything about the evening was pissing me off. I should have gone directly home after work.

Ava and I watched as the familiar pantomime unfolded. Madam Lucian carefully poured yeast into the deep well she had made in the mound of flour. One by one, Ava presented the other ingredients: unsalted butter, vegetable shortening, salt, milk, and the bottle of raw honey with the floating honeycomb. Without using a single implement of measurement, Madam Lucian placed a bit of each into the well. After she had used each ingredient, she placed its container in Ava's hand. Ava, in turn, would ensure that the item was properly capped or wrapped, and returned to its place of origin.

Ava always had the delicate "fetch this, fetch that" jobs because Madam Lucian did not want Ava's or Monica's acrylic nails in her flour. That's why I had forced myself to be here. Eventually, I would help Madam Lucian with the four-part series of kneading the dough would undergo. It was going on 10:30 p.m., but the timing was not too much off. Madam Lucian's first customers wouldn't creak up the stairs until 2:00 a.m., heralding a steady stream of customers until she closed off about six o'clock.

Thankfully, Monica had ceased milking her sickness. She was on top the stepladder taking down the blender to grind coconut meat to make banana cake. Apart from the water filter, the blender was the only piece of machinery that Madam Lucian allowed, and that was only after Ava, Monica and I had presented a unified front against the metal grater.

I was fearful that the bread would turn out flat and hard because of my negative oomph. Monica cracked a joke that was definitely funny, but my brain refused to tell my mouth to laugh. Madam Lucian offered me a shot of the rum punch she brewed for customers who wanted "one for the road." For the first time, I refused it. She fixed me with her eyes and I took this as a hint to excuse myself from the kitchen table. She sent Ava to warm the filtered water, as she worked the butter and shortening into the flour with her fingers. Surprisingly, she called on me again.

"Come, Valdi, pour the water for me," she said.

Then she leaned over and whispered in my ears, "Did I ever tell you about the day my husband, Mistah Alcindore, died?"

"What you ah tell Valdi 'bout me dere?" Monica asked petulantly as she descended the stepladder.

I giggled. We were about to be entertained with a new story from Madam Lucian's treasure trove of lore. She was attempting to dispel my funk, change my oomph, safeguard her bread.

"Well, girls, I was fifty-six years of age to the day, when I realized that the good Lord was smiling on me. I had walked into the hut, just before sunset, and found death riding Mistah Alcindore. 'Mistah Alcindore, you alright?' I asked, excitedly pulling up his two eyebrows. He blinked, but the scent of death was unmistakable, especially to me who knew that smell well. I hiked up my petticoat, quick, quick and ran down the hill into the village, where I found two of Mistah Alcindore's partners who had just returned from hunting. They were drunk as hell. I said, 'Aye, come. Come follow me to the hut. Mistah Alcindore is deading.' I make them stop in the woods, even though darkness start to settle in, to cut six, fresh, piece of cedar board. By the time we got back to the hut, Mistah Alcindore done begin his death rattle.

"The men started nailing the boards into a coffin and tell me to wash and dress him in the meantime. I soaked a washrag with rum and wiped Mistah Alcindore's face. He would like that. Since I never wanted to touch that dry, bony body ever again, I just folded his one suit and tucked it inside the coffin. At least he could dress himself when he arrived at his final destination.

"I said one Perpetual Light, and a couple Hail Mary, and tell the men to take the box outside. Night had fallen. That man was a *jumbie* in life; he would be a worse one in death. I had to get him in that hole as soon as possible.

"I give the men two shovels and a pickax and by the light of a pitchoil lamp, they started to dig a few footsteps from the outhouse. I make them go to eight feet. All that sweating started to make them sober. They began to talk foolishness. One said he was going into the village to find a doctor. The other one said they needed help to swing the body into the hole. I know exactly the help they needed. I started to quarrel, 'Come; make haste, it almost dark. Hurry up before Mistah Alcindore turn *duppy* on my hands!' The men quarrel back that Mistah Alcindore, who the wind used to blow down regularly, was too heavy for them alone to handle. I went in the hut and bring out a bottle of Mistah Alcindore's oldest bush brew. By the time the cork open and the scent tickle dey nostrils, I hear, 'Yes, we could handle dis wuk.'"

I had turned my face from the dough to laugh, but when Madam Lucian asked me for a last few drips, my hand shook, the jug dipped and water flooded the dough. My heart skipped six beats. I fixed my eyes on the flour, scared to look up at her.

"Holy mother of Christ, Valdi, look what you did! Sit down. Ava, come bring back all the ingredients. Monica, I need more flour from the sack, and bring the strainer to sift some. Valdi, you not sitting yet? Please, on your chair."

Madam Lucian was muttering to herself. "I will have to swing the bread in a different direction, this dough is slack. It's very slack."

I wanted to suggest to Madam Lucian that she drain some of the water from the dough, and add a little flour to fix the rest, but I dared not say a word. She sent Ava for her wooden spoon and stirred until the excess water meshed with the original ball of dough, forming a mass of pap. She left the sticky mess on the board for almost half-hour, sat down and turned on the TV that she rarely watched. Ava and Monica took turns at walking calmly behind her back as if they were going to the bathroom, and *making monkey face* at me. I put my head down, transforming my laughter into muffled coughs.

Eventually, Madam Lucian rose, washed her hands, and warmed a scoop of butter. She poured it over the dough, then dusted the mass with flour. She took the wooden spoon and stirred a bit until the dough stiffened. She sank her hands into the mixture and stretched it on the board. She folded it in half, overlapped that half, and kept repeating the process for almost an hour. Monica came behind her and mopped her brow. We knew all was well when a smile finally touched her lips.

"We must always concentrate on the dough, no matter how much fun we having," she admonished.

"Madam Lucian, what 'bout the rest of the story?" Monica asked, reading our minds.

"What story? Oh, that?" she laughed. "Well, nothing much more to tell. The men took turns filling their mouths with rum, which they squirted into the grave. They did it three times each. Monica, this dough could use a lil more flour."

"Madam Lucian, you ah want this heavy sack again?"

"Yes, and the strainer for sifting; nothing more in the bowl here."

"Madam Lucian, please continue your story," Ava prompted.

"I getting back to it. I tell the men, 'Come on. Stop wasting time. Swing him down or I will do it myself.' Girls, I picked up the rope from the ground, wrapped it around the coffin, and say, 'One, two, three ... swing coffin.'"

At that moment Monica, who was about to put the sack on the kitchen table, laughed so hard, she missed the table and the bag tumbled with the open end toward the floor.

"Lawd, Valdi, you ah trip me," Monica said as both of us grabbed for the sack.

Monica fell. The mistake I make was to stand over her, tears pouring down my cheeks, as she lay on the floor covered in flour. She grabbed my legs.

"Monica, stop!" I screamed. It was too late; I was down on the floor beside her laid out in flour, too. Ava laughed, but stayed far.

Madam Lucian sat heavily on a stool. "The two of you baste good in that flour, I wish I had a pot big enough to drop the two of you in hot oil. Clean it up!"

She picked up her dough from the kitchen table and transported the operation to the kitchen counter.

"Please, sit around the kitchen table and drink beer, sorrel, whatever. Just please stay away from my bread. Madam Lucian needs no help from you three tonight."

It was 5:30 a.m. when I got home, clutching a soft, warm loaf under my arm.

After my shower, I pulled the mirror with the découpage butterfly frame from under the bed. Though Ava had given it to me over a decade ago, it was still in its original wrapping. Back then,

Ava was so excitable.

"It's a découpage mirror, Valdi," she had said, stumbling over the word, as she handed me the package for my birthday.

She was always animated, back before she started college. Ava had said the colorful, hand-painted butterflies in their variety of poses on the frame had reminded her of me.

"Valdi, when we first met you went flitting here and lighting there, gathering what you needed, always talking about making money and getting back into school. Then you suddenly stopped; like someone lacquered you in a spot, like these pretty butterflies," she had said.

Her observation set off a spark in me. I went to talk to university administrators about working out something regarding the thirty thousand dollars in fees I owed. It had to be the fatigue over making bread, and preparing to go out without a wink of sleep, that had me reflecting on such pointless things.

I leaned the découpage mirror on the living room wall, closed my eyes and dropped my towel. I peeped with one eye, and then with both. Both eyes opened wide. So my skin puckered a little and my belly was soft. But the overall view was better than most women I knew who done cross forty. Hell! I had a better body than Monica who not even thirty yet. My skin did not glow like long time, but size wise, the woman was correct I was about a nine, the same size I was when I first step foot in America.

I pulled a chair in front the mirror and sat down. My nipples stood proudly in the middle of my breasts not budging, not even when I leaned forward. I stood again, studying how my waist still tapered, my butt still tight. Neither scars nor stretch marks marred the coat of amber flowing over my body. Not one vein had bubbled to the surface of my skin.

When I was small, people said, "Valdi hard like a *banga seed*," because I never bruised when I fell, while every bump on Delia would turn into a festering sore. Inexplicably, Delia resented me for this, too.

A perfect size nine: the woman was correct. I pulled on the pants with confidence. Madam Lucian had done a good job cleaning the stain with her lavender concoction. I put on a lilac shirt — not spectacular, but workable — then the matching white jacket with the floppy collar like a beagle's ears. Monica had pointed it out in a magazine to prove that that style was back in. I should have bought something new, but it was too late now. It was going on eight o'clock and I had to be in Manhattan dressing the boy by 10:00 a.m.

I put on high-heel shoes and modeled for the découpage. A memory hovered that this suit was supposed to have been worn under my graduation gown. I applied crème to powder foundation, sienna-rust lipstick, black eye liner, berry gold shadow, and April-wine blush. I unpinned the weave. Pretty. Pretty and focused. That's what I used to be. I arranged my face in various ways, striving for pretty and focused, pleasant and approachable, in the event that someone might choose me for a conversation.

I said to découpage, "I infer from your remarks, dot, dot, dot, dot. Did you mean to imply, dot, dot, dot, dot?" Not everyone knew the difference between "imply" and "infer."

Important stuff at a glamorous reception for the who's who of the international literati.

Suddenly, the gray curtain swooped down on me like corbeau 'pon a half-dead, mangy dog. It made no sense to go to the reception and make a fool of myself.

The keynote speaker, a Nobel Laureate from Trinidad and Tobago, would be sure to spark controversy, as some believed that he was only there because he black and from the Third World. Suppose I'm asked a question about him because I black and from the Third World, too? Suppose I'm asked if I don't find his poetry too pedestrian. Or how I would respond to the columnist who wrote, "A first grader could explore his thematic sensibility, without learning anything new besides various participles of the word 'fuck.'"?

The Nobel winner was so much more than that, but could I explain that if asked? My final thesis was supposed to be on him, though I never finished it. What did I write in that paper? I held my head in my hands, and tried to chisel through my calcifying frontal lobe. It was like digging through the charred synapses of a brain after it had been convulsed by a flipping stroke.

I reached for some part of that Valdi from almost twenty years ago who could help me at the party, because *this* Valdi certainly couldn't participate in a conversation about ideas. That recognition made me bawl, even as I bizarrely noted that Monica's mundane promise, that the eyeliner she had insisted I buy wouldn't run, held true. Then, like a rainbow that appears in a cloudless sky, I remember the first line of what was supposed to be my first novel: *At the age of seventeen, Beulah's fifth abortion shocked her body into menopause.*

That was back when everyone thought I would one day win the Pulitzer Prize, the quintessential award for American writers. The joke was: I wasn't even American.

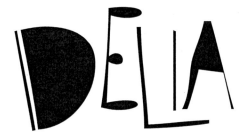

A most dramatic gulf opened between me and myself, when the thought sparked, then exploded: "That's Delia!" as I stepped out of the bathroom with Cole and noticed a woman walking towards me. I knew it was my sister, not because she was close enough to recognize, and certainly not because of some instinctual throbbing in my navel that twinned with hers. I knew that person was Delia because of the metastasizing fear in my belly. The fear that someday, somehow, somewhere, somebody from home would ketch me with one of these white children and make the obvious connection.

In a split second, that fear, flesh out in the person of Delia, buss wide open and spewed, shooting like a geyser up my throat and into my conscious mind. The hallway that was so brightly lit moments ago get so dark that I had to rub my fingers along the wall as a guide to get back into the bathroom.

"Come!" I whisper to the boy, but he say 'no.' He was close enough that I could thrash around with my arms and find him. I grab him by the forearm and push the bathroom door open.

"Why are we back here for? I peed already, stupid." Cole said.

"Come on."

"Rass, no," he said channeling Monica. I held his arm. He pulled away. I had to drag him into the first cubicle. I had barely slammed the door, when I heard the bathroom door open, and heels clipping across the marble floor. A cubicle door about three doors over swung open and closed.

"Shhh," I tell the boy.

"Me say, rass, no."

"Please behave, Sweetie," I whispered.

"Okay."

He held on to the toilet seat and scrambled up. I took out the sanitizer and squeezed a puddle into his hand.

"Don't touch the toilet seat again. Though in here look fancy, it is covered in germs."

"I'm playing something."

"What?"

"Mountains. You come up too, Valdi."

"Shhh."

"But I want you to come up."

"No."

"I'll scream."

I stepped onto the water pipe, pushed him a little forward and stepped on the toilet seat behind him. The top third of my body was over the stall. My face was reflected in the mirror waiting for Delia to see. Panicked, I hurriedly sank into a stoop, nestling in the small of the boy's back.

"Valdi, I'm going to bomb those Islams in the mountains."

"What?"

"I'm going to kilt the Islams in this adventure."

"Don't say that."

He hooked his finger like a trigger. Pretend man push out his chest. Boy, whose pee wouldn't froth even if you done pulse it in a blender, standing on a toilet seat gutting Muslims in his mind. This action sent me spinning back two months to his fifth birthday.

IT WAS EARLY AFTERNOON and I had just opened the dishwasher when a familiar drone warned that the private elevator would soon empty its contents into the foyer. The doors opened; the boy and the asshole roared and stamped their way across the foyer like a writer in Hollywood had scripted that entrance for them. A crash like thunder, and then a scream. Frightened, I dropped the dishtowel and ran to them with my hands on my head.

"Oh God! Who dead?"

Without even a glance at his wife's Matisse lying in a blanket of glass, the asshole grinned.

"Histrionics be damned, you unsightly beast. May no cold water be poured on our celebration of the grand Intrepid."

I asked him if he thought it was right for them to traipse the nasty slush from the street onto the floor I just done mop. The boy dropped his pants and skinned his bottom at me. I *sucked my teeth* and went back to the kitchen wondering if the asshole couldn't find nowhere else in New York City to take the boy besides an old warship filled with weapons and fighter jets. The boy obviously appreciated this early indoctrinating exercise into his "manifest destiny," because he followed me into the kitchen, butt naked, holding his arm stiff like a flagpole with his drawers hanging from his fingertips. He scampered up on the counter, swaggering and bragging.

"We fought the Koreans with the USS-whatever-warship, and kilt everyone 'cept 200."

His pelvis was level with my eye and I see thoughts of conquest galvanize his little pee-pee. I not shame to say the thought of him hardening into a man with these values nearly bring water to my eyes. I shout at him, hearing my voice approaching from a long, long time ago. "Boy," I said. "Get off that counter!"

Then I turn my back on him and the stupid sweating, grunting, grinning asshole and resume my motion: dishwasher, cupboard; dishwasher, cupboard; dishwasher, cupboard; dishwasher, cupboard; dishwasher, cupboard.

I didn't have to look up when the asshole said he was going to a meeting to know the boy was upset; he worshiped that man. I braced myself for the missiles that would come at me once the elevator doors closed, like it was my fault his father was rarely there. The asshole winked at me. He knew that I knew he was off to frolic with one of them dental students he kept in his office. I watched him hard, my lips twisting sardonically.

"If you let me fix those teeth of yours, you won't smile like a crocodile," he said, and threw his business card on the table.

"Call my office. Ooops! You don't have insurance," he smirked, his laughter loud and derisive.

The boy laughed loud and derisively, too.

"Steeeeeeeups. I would never let you near me with Novocain," I said.

I put my fingers on my lips and waved a pack of multi-color, coated chocolates at the boy before the elevator door was even closed. I put two of each color on a big plate. He carefully sucked the coating from each one and arranged them into a pattern.

"Now they all look like you. I don't want them. I don't like you chocolate people."

"We don't like you either. Now, boy, what is a Korean?"

"A martial arts kicker."

"So a Korean is a person?"

"Sort of."

"It's not sort of; say 'yes' or 'no.' Is a Korean a human being like you?"

"Okay."

"It's not okay. Say 'yes' or 'no.'"

"Shit."

"How many times I have to tell you don't use that word? Now answer my question."

"What question, shithead?"

"Is a Korean a person?"

"Yep."

"So, are you happy or sad that you killed them?"

"Oh, shut up, stupid, I said we left 200."

THE BUNDLE OF NERVE FIBERS connected to my spine began to hum, then slumber. As I progressively became stone, I realized I had reacted stupidly in my attempt to avoid Delia. When the fear had screamed that Delia was walking toward me, the return to the bathroom was a good move. But I should have left as soon as she had clicked the lock to her cubicle.

"This adventure is boring." The boy's voice was becoming shrill.

I climbed off the toilet seat, faced Cole and gave him one *cut eye*. He got quiet. I sanitized my hand, and put my last stick of gum into my mouth.

"I want some."

"Your father said 'no gum.'"

"Please."

"No."

Delia flushed.

"I want some. I want gum. I want gum! Give me some gum, please VAL ...!" He was about to scream my name.

I pulled his head down, I brought my mouth to his, and spit the damn gum into his open mouth.

"Chew." I motioned him off the seat.

In the blessed peace that ensued as he experienced his first taste of gum, I witnessed, through a slit in the cubicle door, Delia's kowtow to herself as she repaired her make-up.

Fortune and time had made her stunning. Gone was the Delia of old with teeth like crumbling blue cheese. Her tresses were no less luscious because they had emerged from a plastic bag. Where she had been "too black" under Trinidad's harsh sun and rigid color codes, she was now, at least, a shade above cocoa.

She wore a peach metallic tissue skirt, with a matching jacket that opened to reveal tiny pearls on a chocolate bustier corset. From the way the costume contoured her body, I knew it was designer ... b-i-g designer. I imagined that Delia's suit had once been tastefully arranged on a muted gold Italian leather chaise, the star feature of some Madison Avenue display, strewn with imported orchids and a few delicate accessories. Delia's look, worth at least eight months of my pay, made me feel to end the whole damn joke under the No. 6 train.

It was bad enough to call Papa and hear him talk about nothing else but Delia. Bearing witness with my own eyes confirmed my worthlessness. It's not like I had an overall problem with a Caribbean woman negotiating Manhattan's Upper East Side on business other than babysitting, but why Delia? Delia, who had looked in a picture book, when she was old enough to know much better, and said "fowl" though the letters spelled "h-e-n." Thanks to Papa, I knew about her big job at the stock exchange where she alone decided who would ring the bell to open daily trading.

Papa said that she once met Nelson Mandela. Or, as he put

it, "Mandela fly all the way to America to meet my gyrl."

Papa laid Delia stories thickly like a plush carpet of evidence that proved that I was gum under his shoe. Long aware that to respond only complicated the case against me, I always stayed silent, mentally cursing myself for calling him.

I am illegal in America.

"You was bright, but Delia go win something name Fulbright," Papa said.

I am illegal in America.

"Delia always coming home, and you cyah reach."

I am illegal in America.

"Ah recommending that dey name the Guvment School after yuh sister. Yuh know why?" Posed as a question, as usual, to see if I was listening.

"Why, Papa?"

"Because she went America and make sheself something. She doh fart around like you. Yuh shame meh. You cause me to have to pick and choose what rum shop to drink in so ah wouldn't bounce up dem shit hounds that 'member you. I mean, when they ask 'bout Delia I have plenty ting to say. I say dat she is ah real accountant with sirficate in money, bond, stock and tings. Buh, you? *Ha ya yie!* When they ask what 'bout yuh next gyrl all I could say is, 'She dey.' So what you say is yuh wuk?"

"Writing."

"For who?"

"Freelance"

"What papers is dat?"

"I'm independent."

"Oh ho, so only you reading dat? That ent no real wuk. Dat is what you expect me to tell meh pardners? I'll tell them you wukking for *The Wash'ton Post.*"

Then came the long steeeeups that signaled he was about to slam down the phone.

I was not about to walk out with the boy to give Delia more ammunition for she and Papa to *wash their mouth on me.* If I had been alone in this fancy hotel when I encountered Delia, I could have played like I was something, especially all dressed up like this. Against this backdrop, I would have said, "Delia, I'm here to meet my literary agent and mainstream publisher regarding the impending publication of my novel."

But the boy's whiteness welded on my blackness was the sum total of what I had become in America: a stroller-pusher doing the daily drudge through Central Park on aging knees, stepping and stumbling under the bridges, through the valleys, up the hills, past the rills, shrubs, ponds, swans, frogs, grass, statues, tunnels, squirrels, joggers, cyclists, swings, slides, sandboxes, monkey bars, children, lovers, moats, pastures, fountains, rocks, ducks, fish, algae, geese, hotdogs, ices, food carts and trees. Just a stroller-pusher bent on preserving the image of the American Mammy, as little white dreams rooted and blossomed out of my black, fucking nightmare.

So, on the occasional days I would rise with an improbable spring in my step, a pale leg dangling from any Manhattan stroller affirmed that my literary dreams had fossilized long ago in frigid playgrounds, watching designer children waltz with arctic winds. After almost twenty years, the rationale that babysitting was a temporary means to an end — just something I had to do until I got the money to pay back Columbia University — was the only fiction in a battered, black diary about the day that I took the hamster to the vet, and which job it was that taught me which pesto goes with Australian lamb. In that moment, my sorrow at the improbability of it all burst like gall on my tongue.

My America was peeping at other people's Kodak moments at play dates, in playrooms and parks, feeling like wet bread. My America was the grinding minutiae of dreams unfulfilled.

DELIA FINISHED HER TOUCH-UP and left the bathroom.

"I don't want to do this game," the boy said. "Stupid. Stupid! Stupid game!"

He bent his head and butt me in my belly. His face was purple with rage.

"Ass. Like the stupid mountain game. Stupid. Stupid. Stupid. Stupid. Stupid. Bitch. Ass. I could fire you right now. You are fired. I am your boss; my Dad said so. I pay your celery. I pay your celery."

He spit the gum back at me.

My fingers around his neck and blood seeping from every orifice of his body. The front page with my face; M-O-N-S-T-E-R written in red on my chest, and my lips, nose, eyes and ears all at strange angles like they trying to run. I see myself shuffling to the defendant's box trying to explain how I come to squeeze the air from his windpipe that day. I say how it started when I rejected an offer of a Trinidad and Tobago government scholarship to study for my Master's degree in the Caribbean in favor of a private firm's offer to study at a foreign university of my choice.

I had stepped off the plane on American soil at twenty-five with an honor's degree from the University of the West Indies, a bona fide student visa, and a check that covered my first semester's tuition and room and board at Columbia University. By the end of the first semester, I was showing these American students that they not fit to wipe the shoes of Caribbean students.

Then the private firm that paid my scholarship installed a conservative board that promised to end "wasteful expenditures," which included scholarships at foreign universities. Columbia allowed me to attend on a credit note the following semester. But, after that, what was there to do but withdraw? In a New York minute, I had gone from studying at a prestigious institution to babysitting and playing with little white children, by the steps of an old sundial, on the grounds of that very institution.

I tell the judge that I had tried and tried to find the past due school fees in the $150 a week I earned to babysit, clean, wash and feel a flabby penis rub me "by accident," every time its owner passed. I say that I lost the job when the man discovered that I, Valdi, read *The Wall Street Journal,* too.

"Uppity!" he had declared.

I tell them that I wait and wait by the sundial, bearing the inscription, *Horam Expecta Veniet* — Await the hour, it will come. I wanted some damn thing to happen to propel me back into the lecture halls and the libraries where I belonged.

I say that there was education aplenty out there on the sundial: my old professors whose glances no longer met my eyes; the old black Southerner who brought his grandson to show him a holy place where he join thousands to protest Vietnam; the stray magazine left 'pon the sundial's steps, featuring a photograph of Columbia alumna, Zora Neale Hurston, who once dreamed of standing on that same sundial and screaming something good about America. On the masthead of that same magazine was the name of a former classmate who depended on me for assistance to complete his research assignments. He was now associate editor.

Yuh think it easy to be illegal in America?

The prosecutor shout, "Irrelevant, irrelevant. Stick to the facts. Say why you choked that innocent, trusting, very charming, curly-haired little boy!"

I tell court how I lost two decades of my life running behind ungrateful little wretches like this one who had the audacity to tell me they pay my "celery." I said I had choked the boy because he happened to be the one I was with the day I had had enough. ✳

I SAT ON THE TOILET SEAT. "Cole don't hit me again. Come, sit down. Yuh tired."

He climbed on to my lap and promptly fell asleep. I waited twenty minutes — long enough to ensure that Delia was gone. I woke the boy, wiped his drool, tucked in his shirt and fixed his tie. I took him to the farther of two exit doors that connected the semi-circular bathroom to the halls.

"You're going out this bathroom door. I'm going out that one," I said.

"Di Di wants you to walk out very slowly like my big, special fella. When you get to the end of the wall, where you see all the people, stand there and wait for me." I pointed to the glass walls between the parallel halls.

"We can still see each other even though we're not walking together."

I made sure to warn him not to say my name or approach me until I said so.

After the boy left, I ran through the bathroom, to the other exit. My confident stroll through the hall did not reflect my terror that Delia could call me at any moment. The boy kept pressing against the glass to make sure I was there. I urged him on with little finger movements. Finally, we spilled into the crowded lobby. I fell in step with him, but I didn't take his hand. When the elevator doors to the penthouse closed behind us, I hugged him tight.

"I love you," he said.

"Me too."

We stepped into the ballroom hand in hand. He was hungry, but there was no sign of the appetizers that were being served when we had first arrived. Shiny, sterling chafing dishes were set out on a table, but they were not yet filled for the luncheon. I told the boy there was no food, and he immediately burst into tears, handing me another problem while I imagined his mother clapping daintily in the adjoining room.

A veteran like me should have known better than to get tangled up socially with these people. When the woman had handed me the envelope with my name embossed in gold, I said, "no, thanks," like I said "no" to so many things she had tried to push on me since I started working for her. She left it on the kitchen table, but curiosity vanquished my good sense. Chloë returned to the kitchen and found me opening the invitation.

"Valdi, I know these names don't mean anything to you," she said, snatching it from my hand. "But these are top international writers. The keynote speaker is the reigning Nobel Laureate. He's from the islands, like you. Preceding him are all noteworthy writers. The program also features several pedestrian amusements that I'm sure you'll enjoy, including an African-American choir."

She said that the event would benefit literacy in Africa, and the ticket, which cost several hundred dollars, was on her. I was surprised by how excited I felt.

"Look at you smile. I knew you would get a kick out of getting all dressed up and going to a fancy hotel," Chloë said. "The Winsford is truly luxurious. Rigal did the marble foyer; Cecioni adorns the halls. This won't mean much to you, but you'll find them pretty. You'll be my guest, of course. Not working."

I snapped to attention. "Will one of your casual babysitters be here to watch Cole?"

"No, Cole is attending my event. His father will be there. It's a Saturday. There is one tiny catch: I will be at The Winsford quite early putting the final touches in place. If it's not too much of an imposition, please stop here first and dress Cole. He looks so much better when you do it. Then you and my men can take a cab over."

"I'll take my own cab," I said.

"Why?" she burst out laughing. "Oh, you think you'll get stuck working. Won't happen; but take your own cab, Valdi. I'll pay for it."

I told her that I would pay for my cab, and thanked her profusely for the invitation, really, really meant it.

I KEPT MY WORD. Though I was tired from pulling an all-nighter at Madam Lucian's, I went first to the apartment to dress Cole. Then I placed him in front the TV and instructed him not to move until his father said it was time to leave. I hailed a cab and went to the function.

Though I kept my distance during the opening mix and mingle, more that once I found myself wanting to go to the boy to fix his pants, wash his hands, order him to sit and behave. But I did not. Not even when he started crying for God knows what. I saw the woman scanning the room, and I, too, looked around for his father.

"Valdi, I'm glad I found you. He's restless; take him somewhere. There's a park across the street. Settle him down."

"It's cold."

"It's almost spring. Go, go on."

"Where is his father?"

"He had something better to do, and I cannot take Cole outside. I'm in charge here."

"Please ask one of your friends."

"I can't impose. Please, Valdi, I don't ask for much. The choir won't be performing for at least two hours. He only needs a few minutes; you'll be back soon. Oh, and take him to pee before you return. It's a great choir, Valdi, really."

With that, she disappeared, and Cole started crying to go to the park.

I gulped down my drink, and marched him to the elevator. As we descended, I had half a mind to take him straight to Brooklyn and let the mother figure out how the hell to get him back to Manhattan. That would be good punishment for dragging me here on the presumption that I had come all this way to hear a choir, when I could have stayed in Brooklyn and listened to the Spiritual Baptists chant and stamp in the storefront church next door. Or I could have just lain down in my bed and remember rosy, long time, Trini women who cussed each other all week but played

Jim Reeves' LPs in unison on Sundays. As pots of dasheen bush and blue crab bubbled on the stove and macaroni pie perfumed the air, melodious voices from each household would collide in the road.

> *Some bright morning when this life is over, I'll fly away*
> *To the home on God's celestial shore, I'll fly away.*
> *I'll fly away, oh glory*
> *I'll fly away, in the morning*
> *When I die, Hallelujah by and by I'll fly away.*

So, while she may have invited me to hear choir and play dress-up, that was not the reason I had come. The invitation with my name emblazoned in gold had provoked weeks of dreams in gossamer images.

The whispers wane as I stroll to the rostrum to collect my Nobel Prize. I take a moment. Courtiers presume it is the drama of the writer overwhelmed by countless villains, stabbing hard at the dream. Lips purse and mouths open wide over the temerity of my "fuck you." It's been hell. It's hurt that spews like fossil fuel from the scrotum of men. It's a father's scorn, and a twin's glory. It's the cower at nightfall, as my soul is battered by tricks parading as dreams. And an unrequited poem bruises a weary pen. It's about fame that taunted and hovered but never descended. Failure. My daddy's word. So I don't talk to him no more. For he smelted that word like asphalt, upon my very soul. I hear whispers of pipe dreams, and I am deafened by its roar. I was destined for greatness, only destiny doesn't know.

NOW WITH CRYSTAL CLARITY, far removed from the darkness of sense-less fantasies, I marvel at how adroitly the Fates had conspired to effect the ultimate revenge: Valdi, the scholar and once aspiring writer, working as a babysitter at a literary reception. If it weren't so tragic, I would have rolled with mirth at the irony of it all. I swallowed the bile creeping up my throat.

A waiter arrives with a cucumber sandwich. I open the door to the adjoining hall. The familiar baritone of Isaac Lown spills into the reception area; the same voice that rises obediently from my audio book to participate in my weekly ritual featuring a well-positioned showerhead. Indeed, he was all that! Tall enough, dark enough, man enough … and bright! The boy follows me inside but, since the stage begins right at the entrance to the door, we cannot get in without disrupting the program.

We back out and run along the outside wall. I pull open a door, but a hotel guard says that there are no available seats but I get a peep at the botoxed and collagened set who were creaming their drawers over my countryman while I stand outside. I speed back to the first door. Stage or no stage I was getting inside.

"Excuse you," I say to a man who pokes his finger in my back as I pass.

He points to Chloë, who waves me out the room. She, I ignore. We reach the aisle where there is a scattering of individual seats, but I need someplace where Cole and I could sit together. We plop down on a piano bench.

The boy puts his head on my lap, but I ease him up. I, too, feel like dropping my head in my own lap over how close I have come to having Delia gloat over my failed life. How does one of the brightest bulbs of the post-colonial era spend a lifetime babysitting? A gray storm rages as the Nobel's voice comes to me in rumbles of distant thunder.

"Good writers draw readers into their lived experiences and cultural baggage that have been filtered honestly through each of the five senses."

The crowd erupts. The sidewall slides back, revealing white-gloved waiters and chafing dishes filled with food. The choir assumes its position next to the piano, and the pianist asks me to move off his bench. I don't have the strength.

He disappears and returns dragging a chaise. He lifts the boy over, and I drag across, stewing like beef in burnt sugar. I want to go back to Brooklyn and leave the boy who is now thrashing wildly on the chaise, screaming and screaming about something. I can't make him stop.

I rest my head against the back of the chair and close my eyes. Almost immediately a vaguely familiar scent of maleness envelopes my senses. A ghost of memory swirls then coalesces. I recall a hard-foot, pubescent boy whose pungent aroma I had inhaled during a coming-of-age, August vacation at my Aunty's in the country. Though I had long since forgotten his name, this smell made me think of tasting rippling muscles under sweet, bronze skin and lying under undulating hips. I am terrified; first Delia, now this?

I peep at him from the corner of my eye. It *is* he ... Isaac Lown, hard-foot, smelly boy, turn Nobel Laureate!

He is standing at the back of the chaise, and leaning over. I am terrified of turning fully to face him in case he recognizes me.

"Whappenin," he drawls in a familiar patois.

"I'm okay," I say, wondering in a fog, if I really did look okay.

"Now, hear this: Ask your mistress if you could take dis boy home. Is ah distraction. It spoiling meh show."

The boy jumps from the chaise and runs off screaming for the mother. I doh want him blabbing things about the bathroom, so I move through the crowd trying to catch him.

"Cole, Cole. Come here, Cole," I call, pelting my voice over the ear-splitting cries of the African-American choir that was crying for "J-E-S-U-S, J-E-S-U-S."

I think I see the mother behind a plant, but she disappears. The boy is a rolling ball on the floor. He yanks the end of a tablecloth, capsizing a chafing dish, sending mushy missiles to the ground.

People are around me, asking, "What are you doing?"

What are you doing?

And that make me laugh and laugh. Long time I doh laugh like this. The woman is next to me speaking low and slow like a 45-rpm record on the wrong speed, and that sound run through me like voltage through a subway rat.

"There's something to laugh at? You, you ... nincompoop! God damit! Can't you do anything right? Don't I pay you to figure things out? Do your damn job, for once."

The room dies. I want to tell her something beginning with "fuck." Instead, I tell her, "today is my day off. You do *your* job."

Nobel is right between us, scribbling shit on a program, culling inspiration from my misery. The woman call me a "dumb foreigner."

"You don't want to go there with me, because you won't come back!" I screamed at her back. "Not because you rich and white means you could treat me so. I'm not standing for it."

Gaping white folks refocus their eyes on their drinks. Brown skin waiters drop theirs to the floor. I need the elevator. I need my handbag. It is on the chaise.

"I'll help you," the Nobel said. He clinches my waist like I drunk.

"My business card is in your bag. I'm going to write your story."

"I could write my own story," I say. "And who give you permission to put shit in my bag?"

I rummage around for the card to throw it in his face.

"Then, write it! Write about a black woman's heart imprinted with stroller wheels. Say why she never meets my eyes as she winds that stroller along city streets. Write about the freedom that comes when she dumps her mask at the end of the workday."

"This look like poetry to you?"

"Then write it raw."

I could have told him that stroller marks and masks stay there until the day come that you could turn your rass to the East River for the last time. I could have told him that these children suck everything from you, and how one day two little boys roar "Cowboys and Indians" so loudly that, for twenty terrifying minutes, I could not see.

I didn't know I had spoken aloud until he said, "That's powerful, write it down. Scribble in taxis, sitting in the park, on the trains. Write everything down and call me."

He escorts me to the elevator and leaves. I was waiting for the doors to open, when the woman arrives with the boy.

"Valdi, take him home."

"No."

"Look, Valdi. We obviously have a few discussion points that can happen on Monday. But Cole needs to be at home."

"I'm going home."

"You know him well enough to understand that he needs a nap. I can't leave, Valdi. I must fix what's left of this. I'll be home as soon as I can. Too bad about the choir."

"Choir?"

"You robbed yourself of seeing the choir."

"I wanted to be with the writers," I said softly.

"The writers?" she asked incredulously. "Whatever for?"

I drag myself into the elevator. She steps in with Cole.

"Watch out for traffic; see that he gets home safely."

I feel a tug. I look down and, with his eyes, he begs me to end the crazy day. He weeps, not the usual crocodile tears, but roiling spurts born in helplessness. His mother smiles smugly.

I walk through the grand lobby with my eyes fix upon the exit. It feels like decades, not hours, since I had walked into this hotel alone and had excitedly feasted my eyes on The Winsford's soaring ceilings, following the shades of pink and blue that surge toward the skylight above. The boy collapses midway into the walk and, after a useless fusion of coaxing and chiding, I accept that he is simply too exhausted to walk. I stoop low to allow him to lean on my back, then I struggle up, anchoring his feet around my waist. No more than ten steps later he falls asleep.

"Awww." A camera bulb flashes.

The doorman flags a cab that enters the curved cobbled driveway. He reaches down and opens the door for the exiting passenger. Who should step out the cab but Delia? Her eyes sweep over me taking in everything. Everything!

"Vaaaaldi!?" she says, stupefied. "Valdi, you are a babysitter!?"

Wordlessly, I turn my back to the open taxi door, stoop low and slide the boy onto the back seat. I get in, push him over, shut the door quietly. The lock snaps.

"Valdi! Valdi, you open this door now. Valdi, I'm warning you! Please, good God! Unlock this door! Valdi, you are my twin. Please. Not you, you of all people? What have you done?"

Delia has her face press against the glass pane next to my seat. I move to the other window. She runs around to the other side.

"Cab driver, please unlock the door. Can't you see? She is my sister!!!" Delia screams.

The cab driver looks at me.

"Park Avenue, between 67th and 68th."

Failure. My daddy's word.
I can't hear myself no more
'Cause he smelts that word like asphalt
Upon a winding road.
I hear whispers of pipe dreams
I'm deafened by its roar.
I was destined for greatness
Only destiny didn't know.

A full bladder rescued me from the pulsating, vapor-shrouded image of Delia's face press up against the taxi windshield. My hand moved toward my cracked lips and I realized that my blouse was slit from cuff to elbow; a detail I imagined was astonishingly important. The blinds were drawn, so I pulled my arm right up to my face and followed a thin zigzag of dry blood from the bend of my elbow to a tiny snip on my wrist. Urine seeping and pooling between my thighs sent me stumbling to the bathroom where I voided for three minutes straight. My cell phone was beeping behind the laundry hamper. Twenty-one missed calls caused me to wonder why the hell I didn't hear dem girls ringing down my phone. I figured it was the low battery, 'cause even the time and date on the phone was wrong.

I left the toilet, shedding my wet pants on the way. I plugged in the phone and switched on the TV to get the correct time. The square box on the bottom right of the TV screen seemed to be ticking in tune with my shoulder. I stared at the box until I could see fine details, such as 59°F and 9:35 a.m., Tuesday, March 19. To believe what my eyes were telling me would mean that three whole days had just up and vanished from my life, including my forty-fifth birthday. It was the fault of the TV screen. Not enough light in Ava's god-forsaken basement.

I grab a pillowcase and pull it over my head like the top half of a *burqa.* Yet, I still recoil from the tiny square of sunlight that peeps through the window at my desperation.

I look back at the TV. The date had not changed. I sit on the frog-skin leather couch. I sit on the floor. I sit at the kitchen table. I will my brain to recall something, any little detail that would explain events in the atoms of time between the taxi's hasty retreat from Delia and this moment that seems to have sprung from nowhere. I feel a violent hunger clawing and scraping my guts. I swing the fridge door open and pull up a chair. I stir a fruit bottom yogurt with my index finger and empty it down my throat. From there I build a highway through both shelves: Chicken wings, dinner rolls, soup, French fries, donuts, scoops of mayonnaise, spaghetti, carrots, beer, strawberries and corn beef; everything fusing into one big bolus.

I pick up my pants from the bathroom, vaguely aware of the patches of moisture sticking to my flesh. I put on my sneakers, and go up the stairs. The sidewalk keeps appearing and disappearing, sending me stumbling along the street. I stand at the corners of Maple and Utica Avenues, staring up the hill towards the subway. I would go to Madam Lucian, but that meant dealing with the immigrants on Utica Avenue.

Just like every other friggin' Tuesday morning, Hispanic laborers were offloading trucks filled with tropical roots, fruit, vegetables and fish at Korean shop fronts. Anxious, middle-aged, West Indian women were already swarming wooden tables that pushed three-quarter ways out into the sidewalk. Bullshit Utica, an unplanned scheme of dollar stores, *roti* shops, nail salons, beauty shops, dollar vans, bars and churches humming with folks forced into thinking about survival every minute of their lives. A golden Haitian mango made me think about the boy who liked to roll them until they turned liquid under the skin before he sucked the delicious nectar from a little hole in the top like I showed him. Promises of mangoes and fry bake and salt fish from Brooklyn usually made him behave.

"Yo, Valdi, I got *The Prowl*."

Pirate was calling me to his tablecloth spread out on the sidewalk. That he had a bootleg copy of a major motion picture a month before it even hit theaters confirmed that Jay Gatsby had nothing on him. Even his cases could pass for real. So, at six dollars each and two for ten, he had plenty regulars, including me.

A quick circle of my finger told him, "Not now."

The finger also attracted the Green Machine who pulled alongside. Green leaned across his voluptuous passenger to ask if I going to the mall.

"Move on. Not now."

"Me nah want you in me van anyway, yuh 'hole face ah look crumple. Like yuh mirror nah work this morning."

I had a flash of him lying down in the snow a few months ago, when police pulled him over because he was plying his illegal taxi business using only a Jamaican driver's license. He sneered as he made a wild U-turn in the direction of the mall.

"Put water 'pon yuh face. Wash yuh mouth. Yuh breath stink."

People like Green, Pirate and all the other ass-ketchers on Utica Avenue made me yearn for a decent place to live among little, white shoemakers, shopkeepers and pharmacists. The kind of place that Ernie, Bert and all the other *Sesame Street* puppets would be proud to sing about. I hold on to my belly and howled at the thought of dem puppets trying to sing about Utica Avenue, because an honest song would go something like this:

> *The DVD pirate comes around*
> > *With movies from the underground.*
> > *He copy and wrap dem just like new*
> > *And bring bootleg movies right to you.*
> *Yes, dey are de people in meh neighborhood*
> > *Tasteless neighborhood*
> > *In meh neighborhood.*
> *Yes, dey are the people in meh neighborhood.*
> > *De people dat ah meet,*
> > *when ah walkin up de street*
> > *Stupid people dat ah meet each day.*
> *Green machine will always pick you up*
> > *Then break lights and dodge traffic cops.*
> > *Pay a dollar and then ride in fear*
> > *Cause he drive like he doh fuckin' care.*

I was laughing hysterically by the time I reach up the hill, prompting the crazy fool who was standing on one leg in the middle of the hectic intersection brandishing a giant cross to watch me like I crazy. I didn't care because, unlike him, I knew what was what. I knew I was ketching my ass, seeing trouble. Unlike the smiling gapers and gawkers around me, I knew that Valdi did not come all the way to America just to live among West Indians and make Koreans rich.

"Kings Mall, Kings Mall. Yes, you I talking to. Whappen, yuh stupid or what?" a dollar-van driver ask me.

"Is yuh mudder whey stupid," I say, and that start a cuss-a-thon that didn't stop until I disappear into the subway.

Transit workers stood milling around as I paid my fare. Since it never seemed necessary to dispense info in the black parts of Brooklyn, they didn't bother to tell me that the train system was screwed up, and a wall of frustrated commuters was packed in the pit of the station. I decided to go to Manhattan anyway and, because of this, I killed a man.

THE BALL WAS SET in motion when a No. 3 train rolled into the station, heading up West Side Manhattan. Though I had intended to take the No. 4 train to 59th/Lexington, which is just by Sherman statue, I boarded the No. 3 train to escape the crowded platform.

Everyone obviously had the same idea, because the sheer press of the crowd propelled me straight into the last available seat in the carriage, sandwiching me between two heifers. They were obviously together because talking came at me from right and left. I offered to switch seats, but they wanted to stay put and coat me with spit. Clearly, I was the meat in a babysitter sandwich, an East Side prosciutto inside West Side white bread. They rocked fingernails that curled, sported gems from weird lobes, kaleidoscopic weaves and glued-on eyelashes.

The dark one had three gold teeth from she *jamet* days. The red one had about thirty earrings ringing each ear. The accent told me they were bad gyrls from home, what Monica would have been in ten years.

I wouldn't hire dem to watch a fish, but some liberal had looked somewhere between color of skin and content of character and found them a worthy influence for a child. They returned the favor by bad-mouthing their employers for the whole damn ride. The dark one fussed that the train was slow.

"She going to vex if I reach late again."

"What? The train is yours? You don't control that. Gyrl don't fight up yuhself over dem people you know; dey business alright."

Talk about lateness and trains expanded to "the people" personal business. The red one said how she madam so untidy she just walks out she drawers and leave them there.

Fascinated, the dark one say, "eh heh, hear nuh. You do the laundry too?"

The red one nodded.

"So how you handle dat, gyrl?"

"Meh dear, I just scoop the drawers with a pot spoon and march like a flag bearer to the washing machine."

Both of them exploded in a scandalous piece of laughter that caused me to wish I had a newspaper to read to show I was not associated with them. I could tell that everyone was listening. Some were smiling openly. Churchwomen pursed their lips tightly.

"What you name, sweetheart?" The red one asked.

I cringed as I sat there trying to figure out whether or not to answer. Then the next one said, "Freda."

So all this talk about the employer panties and so was between two women who had just met while waiting for the train! I wanted to get up, but there was nowhere to go. People were jammed up against my legs. The train stalled in the tunnel somewhere between Nostrand and Franklin Avenues, trapping me in this roiling wave of immigrant humanity — wood hewers; water fetchers and paper shufflers; babysitters who raced children in the park and wrapped diapers around hairy bottoms; handymen who delivered groceries and trembled on scaffolding; everybody braced only by a novena.

I was suddenly floating above everyone although I could still see my body sandwiched between them two babysitters. My hearing and my sight were acute; I could take information straight from people's heads. The lady opposite asked her companion for a portion of his welfare check to pay the rent.

Why de hell yuh doan pawn yuh mudder-ass gold teeth? he ask she in his mind.

A boy peddling chocolate bars from a box begged folks to buy to keep him off the street.

But imp, you already on the street 'cause the morning barely ripe and you not in school.

The lady who was purchasing two bars with a loving smile on her face was thinking that.

Then a reeking, hulking vagrant, smelling like fresh vomit entered the carriage bringing me back to earth with one whiff. Coated in sores, he pleaded for food or money in a soft polite voice. Everybody pushed up against each other to give him a clear road. Not one cent went into his outstretched hand because no one was getting that close. He stood in the middle of the carriage and told his story until his voice broke. He dropped to his knees and wept, earning nothing for himself but more space. He rose and pushed his way to the end of the carriage rubbing against as many folks as possible. Commuters screamed and begged as he delivered hugs of absolution. Just before he walked through the connecting door, in a booming voice, he asked God to bless "this bunch of greedy motherfuckers."

As the train crawled along, a teenage girl scored two fists from her man in front their four children and the whole train. A preacher woman screeched down the blood of Jesus on everyone. She had a lot of listeners. Even Red and Black fell silent. The ratio of this part of the journey was 2:4:23: two laptops, four briefcases and twenty-three bibles. So many could follow the preacher woman as she preached about proving God by citing Jonah who waited until the appointed time to climb out the whale's belly. Daniel waited until the appointed time to climb out the lion's den. The children of Israel waited until the appointed time for Moses to unlock the sea. I wondered if she was illegal, too.

The complexion of the train began whitening as soon as we hit Eastern Parkway/Brooklyn Museum Station. Three black women exited, five white women entered. Could it be that that's why the museum now had water in a fountain that danced to Mozart? Was that the reason the pizza man — who had gotten rich making black children fat with cheap cheese, cheap sauce and white flour — now evicted whole black families from above his store, replacing them with "good" white families deserving of gourmet cheese and sauce?

The No. 3 train inched closer and closer to Manhattan: Grand Army, Bergen, Atlantic, Nevins, Borough Hall, Clark, and Wall. More briefcases, more laptops, less bibles. Red's hand was snaking up my thigh. I jumped up just as the train pulled into Fulton Station and everyone was asked to leave.

I studied the subway map on the wall in the station and decided to take the "J" train that ran from Queens to Brooklyn with one stop in Manhattan at Chambers Street where I could transfer to the No. 6 and take that to Sherman. But when yuh sour, yuh sour. So after the "J" train left the station, the conductor announced that the No. 6 was not running and commuters who wished to go up the East Side should get off at Chambers and catch the bus. That's when I decided to stay on the "J," get off at Alabama and catch the No. 12 bus back home. As I leaned into my lap to call sleep, I felt the floor vibrating.

A pencil-sized Mexican was bouncing in the aisle wearing a flowing purple gown with starched pleats. He pulled the gown tightly around his taut backside, wiggling and trembling to a salsa mix that seeped out his headphones. Dancermigo gyrated mostly in front my seat as I had somehow scored a whole seat in a standing room only train. He bumped me a couple times and I didn't even mind, 'cause this madman was free.

After the first couple dances, I offer him money but his dancing was for himself, not for gapers like me. He glided over to the connecting door and yanked it open. Through the window, I could see the top half of his body. He didn't enter the next carriage but, instead, stood between the cars, swaying and bobbing in the wind. He was mad but not stupid, because he held on to a metal strip above his head with both hands. I didn't once move my eyes off him in the thirty minutes it take for that train to arrive at my stop, Alabama Station.

After I got off the train I waited to see Dancermigo on his way. The train lingered on the sun-drenched platform for a few minutes before pulling off. "You're a great dancer!" I screamed.

Startled, Dancermigo let go of the metal strip just as the train lurched forward. He slipped neatly underneath, pliéing to his death. It was a sensation the driver seemed to know. He screeched to a halt halfway out the station as Dancermigo's head pitched onto the platform and landed by my feet.

For a moment I didn't move. I was telling myself that this was a dream on the couch, because nothing like this happens in real life, not even to me. Then I heard screaming. I peeped between the tracks to the street below and followed fingers back to the rest of Dancermigo's body that was dangling between the rails. A transit worker ran up to the platform toward me like he intended to ask what happened. I slinked down the stairs to Alabama Avenue.

"Hey, you!" I hear him calling, but I didn't have to be involved in other people stuff like that. So I crossed the big, wide avenue and melted into the crowd at the bus stop, even as they left me for a front pew view of the unfolding events.

Dancermigo's body tumbled obligingly through the air, bouncing off a car and under its wheels.

It was going to be a long walk to my destination.

THE GIRLS

"Vaaaaaldiiiii! Ah what you ah say?" Monica's scream nearly buss my eardrum.

I pressed the speaker button and slid the phone to the other end of the center table.

"Uh huh."

"Good Gawd. Stay right there. Don't 'ang up. Aavaaaaaah, Aavvvvvvaaaaaah. She nah hear me. Madam Lucian, send your bwoy to call 'er back. Tell her I 'ave Valdi 'pon the phone. Valdi, does Ava need to go to your place and look after you?"

"Don't send Ava here," I mumbled.

"Okay, Madam Lucian send wan bwoy quick! Now Valdi, what 'appen, gyrlfriend? We ah worry. Ava leave the twin with us to go Brooklyn and see what the 'ell up with you. We see you on Friday night. You leave good good to go to that party with your boss. Saturday, my phone ring off the 'ook about 'ow you ah *gwan* in the

'otel. Sunday, we ah try to find you to buss a lime, as onno Trinidadians ah say, to celebrate birthday. Nobody nah 'ear from you. Gyrl,
ah where you was? Why you nah call?

"Monica."

"We ah call, and call and call."

"Monica!"

"You ah make we worry, worry, worry that something drastic
ah wrong. Uncle Ram even ah knock 'pon your door. Madam Lucian wonder whether Ava should call officer, but Ava say she sure
nothing wrong with you. But when she self see Sunday pass ... ah
no you. Then Monday pass and ah no you ..."

"M-o-n-i-c-a."

"And now ah Tuesday come and ah no you, she leave Sherman
step and say she ah go and check 'pon you. Valdi, she ah just just
leave here. You self ah 'ear me ah say to Madam Lucian, 'Send
one big bwoy to ah call back Ava. So you ah where? Buh you nah
say nothing. You don't say nothing. Ah look, Ava ah reach."

Ava took the phone. "Valdi." Disapproval. "Here we go again."

"I was speaking to Monica!" I said sharply.

Without another word she gave the phone back to Monica who
just picked up where she left off.

"Valdi, you ah quit or Chloë ah fire you? 'Ow her face look when
you say 'ow you nah wuk on no fucking plantation?'"

"I didn't say that."

"Yes, you ah say that. Wan babysitter ah say it to my own
two hears."

The idea that my statement had undergone such a drastic
transition suggested that the true facts had had a long, hard slog
through the migrant patch. Word of the incident had probably
crashed through The Winsford's staff doors long before the first
guest had even walked out the front door. My drama had spilled
down the gray, back-of-the-house staircases transmitting virally
through servers, moppers, bellhops, laundresses, dishwashers
and along brown mildewed corridors, into greasy elevators and

then burst like a mortar through the back doors to the lips of babysitters and servants pushing strollers and running errands in Central Park. The hewers of wood and fetchers of water had put my business on the street.

"Valdi, me ah ask you if you ah quit or Chloë ah fire you? So 'ow the whole thing start? Madam Lucian say dat you should come 'ere make we see that you okay. It's wan o'clock. The sun 'ot, so we ah take the children museum. If you leave Brooklyn now ... you ah dey in Brooklyn, right? You ah reach museum by half two."

"Monica, I left the house to go by Sherman this morning, but the trains bad. I had to make a damn circle to get back to the apartment. I not going back out."

"The trains ah bad? Madam Lucian, oh gawd de trains ah bad. Okay, Valdi, you meet us at Sherman tomorrow. Me 'ave to show you wan ting. Gyrlfriend ... look 'pon this bwoy! Oh Lawd, bwoy look 'pon you! Madam Lucian *dust dis bwoy bottom* for me, please. I nah say don't sit down in wan muddy grass? Go to Madam Lucian and ah get your bottom dust. ... Yes, Valdi, yesterday your madam ah show up inna the park with wan gyal that look no more than thirteen."

Madam Lucian's voice rose in the background.

"Alright, alright, Valdi. Madam Lucian say the girl ah look older dan dat. Chloë brought the girl to the statue and say she is the new nanny. She asked fuh us to exchange numbers with 'er new nanny so 'er bwoy still ah play with him friends. Well, flat out me ah say that this phone bill ah mine, ah me pay it and if she want to make play date she must call the phone that my bwoys' mudder ah pay. Madam Lucian tell her that she nah 'ave cell phone. Well, you know Ava, she ah cut her eyes 'pon us and ah give Chloë her digits."

Monica's voice dropped when she mentioned Ava, who was probably nearby scanning the conversation for SIGECAPS.

"Monica doh forget that Ava's jewel-crusted cell phone come from her boss, so she must give up dem digits."

"She ah want to." Monica laughed. "Valdi, come tomorrow. Me ah show you everything. The nanny, ah blonde blonde like ah Tiger Wood's own."

I felt like a beat up old jalopy that was replaced by a shiny convertible. Though I agreed to join Monica, in principle, I was determined not to go. But, maybe, I like punishment, 'cause five past one the next day I was giving Sherman the usual perfunctory glance.

I nearly pee when the horse rear and spin round to face me. Sherman sail right off the concrete platform with Nike flying above him. I gone from Central Park South to the Civil War South. Sherman fire his gun and the place get dark and smoky as plantations crackle and burn. The Confederates secure their flags, then their children, and run 'cause Sherman scream, "Fear is the beginning of wisdom." I see some niggers hiding in the bush and, like them, I don't know whether to run or stand up.

Yankees stand on the sidelines and cheer as the South turn to ashes and the Union is saved. Monica call my name in the dark and I know I suppose to lift my feet and go to her, but I not sure 'cause the children run off. As I stan' up contemplating these things, I hear Monica call my name again.

"VALDI!"

I slipped behind a nannyberry bush midway into the plaza.

Monica touched my arm, "Valdi, me 'ere. Gyrl, what ah 'appen to you?" She brushed her nose ever so slightly.

"Look 'pon your 'air. Come ah make me use this tiehead."

Monica took the scarf from her neck and made an elaborate head tie. Then she dug into her pocketbook and came up with foundation and a pack of feminine wipes and attacked my face. She worked silently for a change, and her touch made me feel okay. She was still quiet as we walked to Sherman who was back on the platform like nothing had happened. I could feel her stealing glances at me. Her boy and Madam Lucian's own were kicking flowers off their stems; she didn't tell them to stop. As usual, Madam Lucian was sitting on the steps with her head inside dem house plans. Ava wasn't there. She was tired of the company and had taken the twins to someplace of educational or cultural refinement.

Monica's phone rang, and when she saw the number she delivered one of those long, hard steeeeups reserved for her employer.

She listened for a minute, then she barked, "ah now you ah call 'bout that? Rass, no! Hif you know dees bwoys have to see wan doctor, why you nah keep the baby girl home this mawning?"

Soon they were arguing, with Monica accusing the woman of always pulling some last minute shit. She hung up in a snit and say how the woman called to tell her the boys have dental appointments cross town in twenty minutes.

Monica was disappointed that she wouldn't be present when I see the girl for the first time. She asked me to leave and return when she was available. I said I was there already and I would hang with Madam Lucian. Monica gathered the boys and left. Madam Lucian squeezed me tight, and her breasts smelled like bread.

"Sweetheart," she said softly, "I was really worried when you did not answer your phone. How you doing?"

Her sorrow made me feel bad for myself, but I say something funny. She selected a photograph from a pile on her lap and asked me to pinpoint that room in the blueprint.

"Boyo sent these, but I can't remember a room shape like a triangle. Can you?"

I said that, in the Caribbean, builders don't bound to follow specs and plans, and even though the room shape weird, the house was beautiful even without one coat of paint.

"With the size of that house, you don't even have to go in that room," I said.

Madam Lucian laughed heartily, because she always got a thrill from hearing about the bigness of that house. Her voice dropped. She said how she feeling bad that she couldn't go home and see her house.

"I fed up with pictures. I want to rest my cheek on concrete," she said.

Tears crept to the corner of Madam Lucian's eyes, and it come to me that babysitters mourn a lot.

"Don't tell me you mean concrete in St. Lucia? Madam Lucian you out of order for crying like that," I said mischievously. "If you cross that Caribbean Sea before time, you can't never come back here and sell no bread to buy fancy stuff. Remember, you do not live in New York or Washington or Idaho or Vegas, you live in Illegal, the fifty-first state. Madam Lucian, as a representative of the United States of America I, Uncle Sam, hereby pronounce you an Illegal-American."

Madam Lucian was laughing now. "Valdi, I'll never forget you called me an Illegal-American like that's some real kind of American. I can't wait to tell the others."

When Madam Lucian laughed, she shaved at least two decades off her age. She liked to say that she looked so young because she didn't start life until "Mistah Alcindore-who-bought-me-for-two-bags-of-rice-and-a-sack-of-flour-at-fifteen-dropped-down-dead-and-left-me-without-a-cent."

Madam Lucian's contempt for Mistah Alcindore starkly contrasted with her feelings for her beloved Boyo who "gave the American visa, plane ticket and one thousand U.S. dollars" that brought her to America. She said her life started in America, as it was here she learnt ambition.

When I first met Madam Lucian, she had already bought half acre, and was designing the house via phone card. Her happiness was infectious and, for the last four years, we all helped with the running around to wire money for bricks and shop for stuff like O.K.K.O. tiles and a bright red Slixxy-Slixx marble counter.

Through photographs, we witnessed the building of Madam Lucian's dream … brick by brick.

The secret, she claimed, lay in the crucifix she rolled between her fingers as she recited her Rosary. Sometimes, she would make us join hands as she prayed for long life so she could enjoy the house. She prayed that we, her "daughters," would accomplish our dreams too: "Ava to finish school and get a big-job; Monica to get the papers and be reunited with her three chirren; and for Valdi to fulfill the big desires of her heart, whatever they may be." Boyo got the most prayers. She thanked God for using him as an instrument to make a way out of no way. She thanked him for Boyo's honesty, and asked that God-Manifest would shower Boyo one hundredth fold and even one thousandth fold.

"If it wasn't for you, Lord," Madam Lucian intoned, "I would be dead and gone without making one mark in the sand. So thank thee, Lord, for hope and breath, and thank thee, Lord, for daily bread. Alleluia. Amen. Hail Mary."

Madam Lucian was staunch Catholic, but prayed with Spiritual Baptist fire. She never lost an opportunity to use the house as a metaphor for prayer changing things.

"It could work for you, Valdi, who don't seem to let 'amen' pass your lips," she would say.

She always discussed major decisions with us and waited until we were together to call Boyo concerning the house. She would tell him, "My chirren here, too. Go ahead and talk."

Madam Lucian said if any of us wanted to live in St. Lucia, she would will us the house because Boyo have more than enough, and she didn't have any family left that she cared about. We laughed and predicted that Madam Lucian would outlive us all. Looking at this latest set of pictures, I marveled at the work ethic of St. Lucians. It would take years for a house like this to go up in Trinidad, where workmen scarce and lazy. The house was not only grand, but also pretty like Madam Lucian. I reached for words to convey the happiness in my heart, but it exploded into thoughts of dreams turned to dust and pushing through a fog. Madam Lucian said how my face dark, and say I should check my blood pressure.

"My health good. When you leaving?"

She put her arms around my shoulder. "By next year Easter I want to be home so Father could bless the house after Mass."

The fact that we had less than a year with Madam Lucian explained why I could find no joy in her good fortune.

"Now, I just need to save for furniture and little money for food," she said.

Ava appeared suddenly. Pointedly ignoring me, she went straight to Madam Lucian waving her graduation cap and gown. She pulled two tassels from a small satin bag and twirled it around the cap, then briefly plopped it on Madam Lucian's head, "For good luck." Madam Lucian asked Ava why she had two tassels.

"The red tassel represents the Department of Psychology, which is presenting me for graduation," Ava said, her backed square to me. "The gold tassel signifies I'm graduating *summa cum laude*."

"What's that?"

"I have concluded my studies with the highest marks," Ava said.

Madam Lucian started telling Ava how proud she was of her. I wished the boy were here to give me something to do. Madam Lucian's eyes darted between Ava and me.

"What happen, you two not talking again? It's time you cut that out, we don't have much time left. Both of you could do better," she said curtly.

Monica appeared with the boys and shooed them off to play with the others.

"Monica," I said gratefully, "what you doing back here so soon?"

Monica said that the boys' mother called while they were almost across town to say she had cancelled the appointment; then she hurriedly turned to Ava.

"Gyrlfriend, put on the gown let me see," she said.

I felt for my graduation ring from the University of the West Indies to remind myself that what Ava was about to do, I had done years ago, and education never, ever got stale.

Ava slipped the gown over her head, and I said very quickly, "Ava, you look nice."

"Thank you, Valdi," she said in a hoity-toity, show off way.

Madam Lucian offered to pay for Ava's graduation hairdo; Monica chimed in that she would pay for nails if Ava promised to wear open toe shoes. I couldn't think of another personal need I could offer to pay for other than a cake of soap to wash Ava fanny, so I keep quiet. Ava thanked Madam Lucian and Monica by name to show me up. She said that she didn't need the help because her family had already given her three thousand dollars to take care of her personal expenses.

The breezes rippled around Ava and her gown billowed. Monica touched the satin lightly and her face filled with pride.

"Ava, they put me outta school at fourteen after I make the first baby, but you inspire me to want to learn something."

Ava hugged Monica and promised to help her prepare for the high school certification exam.

"Ava, you receive any responses from your interviews?" I asked.

I wasn't really interested, but to sit there and say nothing seemed stupid.

"Almost everyone has offered me a position, but I am still waiting to hear whether the Board of Education has a vacancy, because I do not want any position that starts before September," she said.

"Why? That's months away." Madam Lucian said. "This hard work can't end too soon for me."

"That's because you don't have a family like mine. I want to be there when my girls start their first day of real school." A hurricane of tears swept down Ava's face and I fly in a rage.

That heifer just didn't get it.

"Ava, tell me what the fuck you crying for, eh? What it is you really crying for?"

Madam Lucian went pale. Though Monica and I used the hard-core stuff, and Ava occasionally used soft-core cuss words, we never cussed in Madam Lucian's presence, except when I called the man "the asshole."

"Madam Lucian, sorry," I said feeling like the ground should open up and swallow me.

I buried my head in her lap. She struggled to find words of absolution, but Ava had plenty to say.

"I must cry because, unlike you, I appreciate people!" she screamed. "I've been with my family since I was seventeen years old and Ann was sixteen. Although Ross wanted someone experienced to assist his pregnant young wife, he took a chance on me and they were never selfish. They funded me through school, applied for my Green Card, bought me a car, took me to Broadway, exposed me to things. Where else would I be but standing with my family when Ross Jr. went into the military, Timothy to Oxford and Laura to Dalton? In September, I could kiss the children goodbye with my head high, showing the same grace they have always shown me. Valdi, it's called loyalty."

Nobody said anything. Ava slumped next to Monica who was seated next to Madam Lucian, who was seated next to me. Soon, Ava would sit behind a big desk, Madam Lucian would sit in her verandah, Monica would sit in her Green Card interview. I would still sit at Sherman's feet. The woman chose this moment to step into the scene, armed with her new nanny.

Monica had not exaggerated; the girl was really a very blonde blonde. Though I usually couldn't tell whether a white woman was pretty or not, there was no mistake to make here. She had milky skin and sky blue eyes; her hair could star in a shampoo commercial. She had a body like a stripper and she glided like there was a red carpet beneath her feet. Ava shot me a look that meant "behave." Monica stretched over Madam Lucian and nudged me to make sure I was watching. Madam Lucian put her hand on mine for restraint.

I hoped they would pass straight. As she circled the monument, the woman spoke loudly, extolling Sherman's values. Monica talked loudly to shift my attention, but the woman wanted me to see, so she descended on us with one arm around the boy and the other around the nanny.

"Oh, Valdi. This is Aleksandra from Russia. Alex, this is the old babysitter."

She had once told me that when introducing two people, the lesser ranked gets introduced to the greater first. It wasn't lost on me that she didn't call my name in the introduction.

I held out my hand, but stayed sitting so the girl would have to bow to shake it. The woman asked the boy to give me a hug, as though I must want one. He wrapped himself in his new babysitter's skirt.

"Good-bye," the woman said smugly.

Monica touched me and mouthed, "keys."

"Wait for your keys."

"Keep them. I had both the lock and the elevator code changed," she said, not bothering to turn around.

"What about my money for working Saturday?" I said, scrambling to my feet and flying toward her.

"Oh God," Madam Lucian moaned.

"What about my money for taking advantage of me?"

The woman noticed outsiders' eyes focused in our direction, their sandwiches frozen in mid-air. Perhaps fearing a repeat of The Winsford, she peeled off some bills and passed it to the nanny.

"Pay her!"

I snatched my money from the girl hand while extending my

other hand with the keys, but she walked off without taking them. Suddenly, the anger that had seethed and boiled, making me want to slam that woman head on the concrete step, dissipated.

I laugh, and laugh, and laugh, holding my belly to protect it from pain. Monica and Madam Lucian begged me to share the joke. What was so funny enough to send water running down my face? I couldn't even speak to tell them that it wasn't funny at all; that the woman had imported trouble all the way from Russia, 'cause there was no way that the asshole could do without a piece of that!

BACK THERE AGAIN

About a month after I lost the work, I started looking for a new situation 'cause rent don't pay itself. Monica and Madam Lucian told me about jobs, and Ava sent leads through them, since we were not speaking, but the money was short and the hours long. Those jobs suited women who come to America on a six-month hustle to fill a barrel and go back South. I resorted to an Internet nanny site, though I preferred word-of-mouth situations where I could check out the family before I got involved. I titled my post, "Supernanny Available." I moved my cursor back and changed that to "Educated Caregiver Seeks Suitable Family." I published my posting, boiled water for coffee and waited. Not even fifteen minutes had passed before the first ding alerted me that a response had been delivered into my mailbox. Within the hour I had forty responses, and I knew plenty more would come 'cause these people get aroused when they find one of us who could make a subject and a verb agree. Plus, my post contained sprinklings of four- and five-syllabic, orthodox, non-threatening words to indicate above-average intelligence. Who wouldn't get high over a posting like this?

> *Dear NYC Parents,*
>
> *I wish to share my copious love and childcare knowledge with a suitable family.*
>
> *I have almost two decades experience as a caregiver, and I take my chosen profession extremely seriously. The special activities I plan for the children in my care reflect my great enthusiasm for literature and the arts. I also promote regular exercise, a healthy lifestyle and limits on snacking and TV.*
>
> *As a caregiver, I have one goal: to facilitate an environment where safety, learning and harmony are paramount. A child's happiness is always my first priority, because I know that if your child is happy, you will be happy, and that happiness will spill into the working environment.*
>
> *I thrive best in a respectful, professional and pleasant working environment. These are my parameters:*
>
> *I prefer to devote my attention to one child.*
>
> *I am seeking a live-out position: Monday to Friday for any eight-hour period between the hours of 7:30 a.m. to 6:00 p.m. Paid overtime can be arranged in the event of an unavoidable emergency.*
>
> *Please do not respond if a dog is part of your family!*
>
> *If you believe that I am the right fit for your family, please reply so we can discuss further. I look forward to speaking with you.*
>
> *Thanks for your kind consideration!*
>
> *Valdina*

By late afternoon, I had reeled in a big fish with a British accent. We set up a time to call. The conversation proved long and strange, because she didn't ask the usual "how-long-have-you-been-a-nanny-and-why-did-you-leave-your-last-job" type of questions. I didn't worry about hours and salary as I could tell she was a liberal. She asked what island I was from, and was excited when I said Trinidad and Tobago.

"You have the nicest people there. I visited your country when I was ten to see my uncle, who served as governor general. It was the most fun I ever had. Though, if you tell my husband I said that, I will deny it," she whispered as a man guffawed in the background. She laughed, too. Together, they sounded like coins dancing on a glass table.

"Is Trinidad still as beautiful?" she asked.

The question made me sad, for I knew about the young boys who chose a gun with eight rounds over a diploma with eight subjects. I always wondered if the nationals that left and never returned cause that.

"Trinidad has American values now," I said to the Brit.

"You speak very well, Valdi. But the comparison is troubling. It always dismays me when an island loses its quaintness."

Because that leaves fewer playgrounds for rich, white people.

"Well, modern Trinidadians associate that supposed quaintness with what one writer — Austin Clarke is his name — terms 'Growing up stupid under the Union Jack.'"

"It is obvious, Valdina, that you did not grow up stupid, and you are a child of colonialism, I gather?"

She was trying to gauge my age.

"Independence came in '61; two years before my birth but, for decades, people still considered England the motherland, maybe because most Caribbean islands were still under British rule. Or, perhaps, it's because Trinidadians always look to that which we consider grander that our own selves for a pattern. We stayed British in thinking for a very long time; and now we're American."

Suddenly this was not even about trying to get a job. The conversation sailed me back to the lecture halls of the University of the West Indies where we would discuss the impact of dominant cultures on small societies such as ours, and the pivotal social choices we would make as the next generation of leaders. Only, I was not among my former classmates who are in the upper echelons of the Trinidad and Tobago government.

The Brit, who turned out to be a housewife and non-practicing anthropologist, was fascinated by this notion that people could "grow up stupid under the Union Jack." So she asked what that meant to me.

I told her it meant standing in the hot sun at eight years of age, waiting to recite a poem for the Queen. I told her about standing on a whitewashed platform in a long-sleeved starched shirt, long skirt, wool cardigan, knee-high socks and tight shoes, waiting for hours for the Queen to grace us with her presence. As my skin blackened in the noonday sun, I longed to be one of the ordinary children, like Delia, who stood waiting in the cool shadows of trees that lined the route the motorcade would take.

THE HEADMASTER and other dignitaries had abandoned the chairs behind me, seeking respite and shade in the rum shop. As the lookout, I trained my eyes up the hill, watching for the motorcade's appearance to signal the dignitaries back to the platform. When my shoulders sagged and the Queen's orchids died at my side, the headmaster sneaked up behind me and screamed: "At-TEN-tion!" His breath smelled like Papa's. I assumed the position: chin up, toes pointed and bowed so low that the red dirt from the floor entered my nostrils. I sneezed.

"Don't you sneeze on the Queen," he roared. "Now say it!"

"It," crawled out my throat.

> *"Hail Britannia, Hail, hail, hail*
> *Thou wondrous empire will never fail.*
> *Welcome Your Majesty to Trinidad and Tobago*
> *Land of the Ibis and the gray Cocrico.*
> *We pledge to you, good mother of our land*
> *For Britain we fall. For Britain we stand."*

I cursed "it" for nesting in my brain. It was this "it" that made me a sun sacrifice. Because of "it," I had won a nationwide competition to wait uncovered in the heat of a brain-addling tropical sun for the Queen. The morning passed and half the afternoon before the motorcade finally appeared on the hill. I signaled. In an instant, the wilting orchids left my hands and bright red bougainvilleas took their place. The dignitaries scrambled to the podium, as the honor guard came strutting down the street. I sang lustily as Britannia's anthem roared from above.

> *"Long live our noble Queen,*
> > *God Save the Queen!*
> > *Send her victorious,*
> > *Happy and glorious,*
> > *Long to reign over us;*
> > *God Save the Queen!*
> *O Lord our God arise,*
> > *Scatter her enemies*
> > *And make them fall;*
> > *Confound their politics,*
> > *Frustrate their knavish tricks,*
> > *On Thee our hopes we fix,*
> > *God save us all!"*

It was a gloriously giddy moment that had been nurtured by

some vague notion that, one day, my name would be called along-side the likes of the revered father of our country, Doctor Eric Eustace Williams. I scanned the sea of ordinary girls and boys and picked out Delia who was happily waving her little Union Jack flag. The motorcade inched closer to *my* moment when Her Majesty would float to the podium, accompanied by the Governor General, to receive *my* curtsy, *my* flowers, *my* poem.

The motorcade never stopped. It just inched by, horn tooting as a lily-white glove waved ever so regally from the cool recesses of an official state car. I could hear myself calling, though my lips didn't seem to move. I pelted the bougainvilleas in the motorcade's dusty wake, and the headmaster broke a branch and whipped me on the spot. I didn't feel a single stroke in the fog of disappointment and humiliation that, at that moment, took up permanent residence in my consciousness.

"What a great story! I'm sorry it worked out that way, Valdi. But it was a great achievement to win a national poetry competition. It must have been extraordinary circumstances that brought you to babysitting. I'd like to hear it one day."

A lump in my throat, scalding tears blistering my cheeks. She knew, 'cause she kept talking, saying how she had her own experiences of Britishness in the Diaspora since she had been born to Brits in South Africa and was raised under the skirts of their Zulu housekeeper.

Mandela's jailing, Biko's murder, tiny-coffins-in-a-line, tires burning. Red dust Soweto slums. Winnie nailed to a cross. Searing images flitted unbidden through my mind like a tableau. I didn't know what to say.

She was feeling me because she said, "Valdi, we are not all the same."

I was not working for no Boer, but I couldn't say that. Instead, I related down to the last humiliating detail what had happened between the woman and me at the literary reception.

"Valdi, why are you doing this? Some employers might think it shows you in an unfavorable light."

"It shows my former employer in a worse light."

"She isn't seeking employment."

"Well, I thought you should know."

"Because I'll be checking your references?"

"Not really. I have friends with white people accents and 212 area codes who would willingly pose as employment references."

"Now, I'm certain you don't want this job. For the record, had I invited you to a party as my guest, I would have treated you as such. I suspect that we shall work well together because I want an equal not a blinking asswipe."

"Good, because, Lisa, I don't wipe anybody's ass."

"Valdi, please let me have your former employer's phone number. Should she give you a good reference on matters related to your work ethic, we can move ahead with an interview."

"What would you ask her?"

"What was good about Valdi? What activities did she plan for the children? Could she draw upon a social network of babysitters for play dates? What were her methods of discipline? Was she punctual? Accessible? How often did she miss work due to illness? How did she handle emergencies? Did the children like her? How would you rate her on a ten-point scale? Would you hire Valdi again … that sort of thing," she trailed off.

"Do these questions make you uncomfortable?"

"Here's the number, make your call, let's see if you pick this up later," I said.

I knew that once the woman was finished vilifying me, Lisa wouldn't be calling back. I wished I had provided a fake reference.

"Oh, what's her name?" Lisa asked.

"She'll answer. Look, I have another call."

"Go on, I'll ring you this afty."

"Goodbye, Lisa."

It was too bad. If I had met her in person, I would have made her hire me solely on vibe. I spent the rest of the morning listlessly scrolling through other replies to my post. Late that afternoon, the phone rang.

"Valdi, guess what?" Lisa was breathless. "You scored an interview, you got an absolutely fantastic reference," she said.

"For real?"

"When I asked, 'would you hire Valdi again?' Her exact words were, 'in a heartbeat!'"

"Did you ask her why I left?"

"She said that she had made a mistake. She didn't mention the incident at the literary luncheon, but I'm sure that's what she meant. Anyway, her loss. Valdi, let's meet tomorrow morning at eleven."

"Noon," I said to make her get that I had a hand in setting the agenda.

I wondered what the hell was going on with the woman that caused her to give me a good reference. She who had found Pilar lacking for buying a pair of boots that was like hers. Lisa had said that the woman took responsibility for the incident between us. I started feeling bad about some of the things I had said about her. I felt bad enough to wait until I was sure she had left the house next morning to leave a message thanking her for the reference.

Then I turned my attention to my interview with Lisa.

I took my time to dress, pairing a white lace shirt with a navy skirt suit, which I complemented with navy blue pumps. I powdered my face and added a touch of functional brown lipstick and a hint of blush. By 10:30, I was on the No. 4 train with my newspaper and pocketbook under my arm, staring at a woman who looked just like Delia. Many people resembled Delia since The Winsford incident, which made me think of Papa crying into his rum about his failure in America who was watching white folk's children.

More than once, I picked up my phone card to call him. But,

the thought of ice clinking against enamel, as he invoked brand, new curses on my behalf, stopped me from doing so. I was cock-sure Delia had done spilled her guts about me minding people kids in America. Thinking about Delia and Papa stirred the fog, but I fought it by opening my papers to sink into the lives of people with more problems than me.

The front-page story had a frowsy looking woman in handcuffs who had supposedly murdered her police captain husband by putting anti-freeze in his evening cocktail. Apparently, the evidence against her was circumstantial until the family of a previous husband she once had in another state told investigators that he had died mysteriously, too. They exhumed his body and found anti-freeze crystals in the casket. I tore out the page and kept it to show Monica who, for sure, would get a kick outta that. I moved on to stories about an Illegal-American, Mexican worker who fell twenty-two floors off a scaffolding and lived; a scientist who invented a new alloy to construct a border fence; and the Big Recession.

Before I knew it, the No. 4 train had arrived at my destination.

I HAD BEEN IN SO MANY fancy apartment buildings in my time that I did not indulge the wow factor. The doorman, a Hispanic with perfect English, asked if I had come to interview for the babysitting job at Lisa Beckham's place. He said that whoever got that job was lucky, because the family had money and manners. I asked him if he knew what had happened to their last babysitter, and he said how she had moved back to Barbados. He said that she had lined up her sister for the job, but Lisa wanted to interview a few people before making her decision. Soon, I was in the elevator heading to the penthouse.

She looked just as I imagined — late thirties with a warm broad smile and heavyset, though her substantial breasts drew focus away from her chunky belly and thighs. We locked eyes for a moment, and then she sent peals of music ringing through the hall.

"You don't look at all like I pictured you," she said, laughing until tears sprang to her eyes.

She guided me through a sunny room that was so large its farthest wall was barely visible. The apartment took up the entire city block. I was stunned. Though I had been in and out of these people homes for years, I had never seen anything quite like this.

"Stupid, isn't it? We call it the big room. Oftentimes I think I married too well," she said wistfully.

"Housekeeping is not part of this job right?" I asked anxiously.

"Of course not," she said.

Again she sent peals dancing around us. "Valdi, you have an acute sense of the sardonic. Don't worry; our cleaning team is huge. Come, look through this window. Isn't the view great?"

She ushered me through the apartment simultaneously excited by and dismissive of its impressive features. The chinky place on Midwood could barely hold the landlady's old yellow couch. At Lisa's, space was abundant, but furniture was an afterthought: worn couches, an old TV, no stereo, a piano, scattered rugs, a modest dining room set. She took me to her son's room, which was painted in the same warm brown of the big room. Well-stocked bookshelves lined the four walls, making it look like the boy slept in a library.

It was use of space that caused white folks homes to radiate a different energy from ours. Lisa had an entire city block at her disposal, but a mere sprinkling of things. Monica, who had one room divided into three, had a wide screen TV where a bookshelf should be and a six piece "Italian" living room set where her children should be running.

Lisa invited me to sit in the dining room, at one of two places set for tea. She picked up a beautiful silver teapot and poured a fragrant berry brew into my cup.

"You do like tea? I'm sorry, I should have asked first," she said, suspending the teapot in midair, anxiety pleating her face.

"Should I take it away? I shall brew coffee, or fetch you a cold drink. What do you want to drink, Valdi?"

"I can't wait to drink this tea; it smells delightful," I said.

Lisa smiled and filled my cup. She pulled her own tea setting from across the table and plopped down into the chair next to me. "Now, my friend, shall we start?"

Suddenly, I was aware of the familiar precursors to the fog: the pulsing shoulder, beads of sweat. I was petrified of blowing this opportunity to work for someone who treated me like somebody. So, even when she said that she and her husband could no longer conceive naturally and were thinking of adopting from China, I found myself willing to bend my "one child" rule. I agreed, consoling myself that Chinese people don't give anybody trouble.

I asked Lisa why she needed a full-time sitter when her son was in full-day school. She said though she needed someone primarily in the afternoon, she knew nannies needed full-time work and she could certainly afford it. She said that I could do as I pleased most days until pick-up time at three. She was talking like the job was mine, and I was thrilled.

"What books do you like?" she asked.

"Well it depends on the child's age, *Mufaro's Beautiful Daughters* is a keeper, the *Spot* series is great for early readers. For a child your son's age ...."

"Not books for children, *your* favorite books," Lisa said.

"That's easy! *A Lesson Before Dying* by Ernest J. Gaines, *Things Fall Apart* by Achebe, George Eliot's *Middlemarch,* which was the first European novel I read. Anything by the Brontë sisters, and *The Lonely Londoners* by Samuel Selvon, a Trinidadian."

"Do you like poetry?"

"Not that much," I was thinking about Mr. Nobel.

"Do you read newspapers?"

"Every day."

"Which one?"

"All three dailies, on the subway back and forth."

She asked what I did for fun, what my family was like (she got the edited version), and so on. She didn't ask a single question about babysitting. Then she asked me to accompany her to meet Benjamin, who, to my surprise, had been in the house the entire time, reading in his father's library.

"I don't get him involved with the interviewing unless it's someone very special on a very, very tiny shortlist of one," she said smiling. "I am so excited about having you join us." She squeezed my hand briefly.

Lisa knocked before we entered the library, and a little voice invited us in. I nearly buss out laughing. Benjamin was seated on a grand leather chair that would swallow most men, with a book on his lap and a big black pipe hanging from the corner of his mouth.

"Benjamin, put back your father's pipe," Lisa said sternly.

A mischievous grin crossed his face, but he got up immediately and put the pipe back on its stand. He had tousled black hair, a handsome face and a ruddy complexion like the pixies in Enid Blyton books. He extended his hand and graciously introduced himself as "I'm-Benjamin-and-I'm-five-years-old-I'm-pleased-to-make-your-acquaintance."

"Benjy, don't speak so quickly," Lisa said, playing with his curls. "Valdi, we'll go to his room where you two can get acquainted while I make some calls in my bedroom."

After Lisa closed the door, Benjamin gave me a tour through his library. He asked whether I like to be read to and, when I said "yes," he asked me to choose a book that I really, really liked. I made a great show of walking along the entire bookshelf twice before I settled on The Raven and Other Tales, a book of African children's stories.

"You picked my favorite book," he said approvingly. "I don't read it that much any more ... look!" he showed me the cracked spine. I asked for glue and tape and carefully repaired the book.

"Thank you, I will read you two of the *Raven's* tales," he said. So I sat on the floor and he nestled by my side and read so proficiently that I stopped him to confirm that he was four.

"Four and one-eights," he corrected.

When he was finished, I offered to read him a tale for his kindness. He nestled under my arm. In the middle of my tale about the young prince who searched and searched but couldn't find a way up the steep slopes of glass, a bell clanged in my head, warning me that we were being watched; that this house was rigged from top to bottom with nanny cams. The tolling soon faded 'cause I didn't care. Lisa had every right to protect her family. I really liked her and I liked this boy and, as long as she did right by me, she could install a nanny cam under my damn shoe.

For two hours I enjoyed this world with Benjamin. I taught him a clapping hand game, and he showed me his very special toy "that only his very best friends can see" — a small silver carriage pulled by miniature horses that looked so real, I refused to touch them.

When Lisa came to fetch us, she was beaming happily and welcomed me into her fold with a warm embrace. Her extra burst of sunshine confirmed the presence of nanny cams. The three of us walked the wide hallway back to the dining room hand in hand. I sat and Benjy leaned on my legs.

Lisa offered me six hundred and fifty dollars a week. She said if the adoption came through, the salary would increase by three hundred and fifty dollars.

"Is the salary acceptable?" she asked anxiously.

"It's more than I expected. I feel guilty. Thank you," I said, pleased that something I did on my own could turn out so well.

"I know you're worth it," she said. "This is the elevator key. I'll go down with you when you're leaving and show you how it works."

"When do I start?"

"Tomorrow?"

"No, Monday," I said.

"Good, the details are settled. Let's get the paperwork out of the way," she said, presenting a form on a clipboard.

"Paperwork?" I whispered, grabbing the clipboard.

There it was, perched dead center at the top of the page: Social Security Number.

Nine gaping spaces that she expected me to fill with the password to America! I glanced up, and whatever she saw in my eyes wiped the giddy smile off her face. I was furious that she wanted to follow the rules. It was the first time in almost two decades spent watching white folks' kids that any employer had ever, I mean e-v-e-r, requested a piece of ID, never mind a Social Security Number, permission to conduct a background check, and to withhold the relevant taxes.

"I'll take my coat. Now." I said, sliding the boy off my lap.

"I don't understand," she said.

"I didn't expect these papers."

"Valdi, it is *just* a formality. The position is yours. I don't even care about this," she said, putting a marker through the background check section as she spoke.

"Please just complete this part; it's the law," she said circling the boxes for the SSN, and the place where I should sign to have taxes withheld.

Benjamin held my leg doggedly, aware that his little boat was capsizing in high seas. Lisa stood in my path, denying me the opportunity to at least walk a straight line to the elevator.

"Valdi, I won't do a background check, just tell me if there is something I should know. We've all done things."

"I don't, can't work on the books."

"Oh! Ohhhhhhh," she said. "Why didn't you say that before all this?"

"You didn't ask."

"In your post, you said that you take your chosen profession very seriously, you said it, Valdi. You did."

"You didn't ask."

She took a few steps toward me and tried to pry the boy off my leg, "What bloody hell illegal goes to Columbia?"

("What legal Columbia alum would babysit?")

"Other people can hire whomever they please. My husband is a major Washington powerbroker. Some believe he has a good shot at the presidency himself. He would have my head if he knew I brought you here without the proper vetting. I'm sorry I got so caught up in our talk that I was not careful. We did have a nice talk. I'm sure you understand. We do things the proper way in this family. I should have asked, you should have said ... best wishes."

She pressed my coat determinedly into my hands and, without another word, vanished down the hall with Benjamin who was weeping into a handkerchief.

Monica's call made me teeter on the edge of the stepladder as I reached for the cell phone on the kitchen counter. I was busying myself with some dusty dishes that were on the top shelf of the kitchen cupboard since before this apartment became mine. I answered Monica short, but felt bad when she said that she had been thinking about me all day, and was calling to see how the interview had gone.

"Your stuff have to be in order to work there," I said.

Vocalizing this had brought back a rush of bad feeling.

"So why she nah say that from up front?" Monica said, launching into the real reason for her call.

"Valdiiii, I 'ave wan 'ot coal for you. You must plant you rass 'pon wan chair for this. Did you plant your rass 'pon a chair?"

"Just talk, I can't sit now; I *washing wares.*"

"Then I will rest it 'pon you standing up."

Monica liked to make them rude jokes. I never laughed, because I didn't know which side of the fence she was leaning.

"Monica, I have another call," I said, glad to get her off the phone. I glanced at the caller ID. My armpits spring water; it was the woman.

"Monica, you wouldn't believe who on the other line."

"Me know ... Chloë. It must 'ave to do with the 'ot coal me 'ave for you. Gwan, answer it."

"It stop ringing."

"Valdi, you tell wan lie! I still hear the phone ah skip. Answer, and call me back."

The woman kept calling the cell phone and then the house phone. Finally I snatch one.

"What?"

"Valdi. I gave you a lovely reference yesterday."

"And I left you a lovely self-explanatory, crystal clear message saying, 'thank you.'"

"Obviously, you are still miffed over the fiasco at the party, but I am calling to extend an olive branch."

I told her that I don't like olives and she said, "After a relationship of four years, we share a great deal of common ground."

"Which we covered already. What is this call about?"

"Valdi, I need you to come back to work." I planted my rass like Monica had suggested.

"Valdi?"

"What happen to your nice young nanny?"

"That is not your business," she said.

Like she gets to decide that! I told her that the whole damn conversation was not my business 'cause I not working for her.

"What can I do to help you move beyond this one unpleasant occurrence to a renewed sense of cooperation?"

I wanted to lace she with all the curses I think up since the luncheon, but being wedged between a rock and a hard place in America for so long had my eyes wide open. It was a job. Plus, as Mammy used to say after she done complain that the Hammermills had she ironing whole day, "It's better the devil yuh know than the one yuh don't."

The woman was my devil, the one I know. Lisa had turned out to be the devil I did not know. The woman asked if I could meet her in the city. The question was hanging in the air when my other line beeped.

"I have another call."

"Must you take that now?"

"This is my phone," I said.

"Yeah, Monica."

"You still 'pon the phone?"

"Uh huh."

"What she ah say?"

"She want me to come back to work," I said.

"Of course, 'cause you never ah sleep wid 'er 'usband. Ah dat me ah 'ave to tell you. The blonde nanny take away her 'usband. Dem ah live in 'ouse together."

"How is Cole?"

"Dunno, he don't go in the park for days. Now, Valdi."

Monica's voice assumed the familiar authority she reserved for gossip.

"You could choose to take back the work. You could choose not to, nah so? But you just make sure you ah bring back the whole story about the affair."

I was grateful for this information that put the woman's request in context. I now had the upper hand in our latest two-step for a change. Life was usually a seesaw with my backside always on the ground, but the knowledge that she needed me dislodged my tail from the mud and sent me slowly skyward. I agreed to meet in Dinosaur Park on the West Side that same day.

She was sitting on a swing, looking like a fold up *roti*. I passed the figure twice before noticing the feet were encased in the same fancy boots that killed Pilar. I shook the chain on the swing, and

when that head rose I shuddered. Botox should include the dis-
claimer that it totally collapses under the weight of life's miseries.
As bad as the woman might be, no one deserved suffering that
looked like this. Suddenly, what the man did seemed really wrong.

She pointed to the swing next to her and said, "Sit down."

My sympathy ebbed because she spoke like the swing was her
personal property in her kitchen and I was still her servant. I waved
off the seat and stood in front her, forcing her to look up at me.

"I have filed for divorce and moved into a new home with Cole.
My husband and my nanny are screwing in our home."

"Sorry to hear that," I said, surprised at her frankness. "How
is Cole coping with the change?"

"He's having a really hard time. He's the one that found them
... together. His psychologist recommends that I restore as many
familiar connections as possible to maintain some semblance of
security during this upheaval. That's the reason I called you. He's
known you for a long time. Valdi, I hope you'll agree to help. He's
not the same since his father ...."

She threw her hands up and wept, and the wide river that had
separated us receded leaving damp ground. I tapped her back.

"Don't cry. It will work out. I really have to go now. I really hope
things work out for you and your family," I said, my mind firmly
angled toward Brooklyn. It was too much information, and w-a-y
too much involvement.

"Valdi, he needs you."

"Look, children bounce back, they always do. Just give him love.
Many children from broken homes still thrive. Their lives work out
okay. He will be fine. Really."

"If you won't even discuss this, why did you come?"

"I don't know, because I gave my word at the other job."

"What is the salary?"

"Six hundred and fifty."

"A week!?"

She said that like I not good enough to make that money, though I would rest down my neck under a guillotine that she pay the Russian more to service her husband.

"That's over eight thousand dollars more annually than you earned with me," she said.

"Well, you can see how working for you again will be a step backwards," I say, perplexed at white folks' capacity for figuring out the whole money thing fas' fas' and putting it ahead of everything else.

"What in heaven's name are you going to do with all that cash?"

I started toward the road.

"Please, Valdi."

"I gave my word. You'll find somebody."

"My son is out of control. He called me a whore and grabbed a walker from an old lady."

"Was she hurt?"

"A little bruised."

"Then that's not so bad."

"He hacked Peter in four."

"The hamster?"

She nodded.

"Well, that situation too dangerous for me. Find someone who don't know anything about your family," I said.

"I'll pay six hundred and seventy dollars weekly.

"No. Seven fifty." *That was Ava's current wage.*

Startled, I glanced behind me to see who had said seven fifty, because that counter-offer did not formulate of its own accord in my brain."

"Valdi! How dare you try to exploit my situation?" she fumed. I told her that money must correlate with responsibility.

"Understand that I already have a job that I am happy with. My new boss has a son as well ... British. Impeccable manners."

The woman jumped off the swing and come up in my space like the first time she had interviewed me.

"If I am going to pay that kind of money for childcare, be on notice that you are going to be working on the books. This way I can file for a Child Care Tax Credit and other breaks available to families who pay for help."

"I agree totally," I said, not missing a beat. "And I will need a W-2 form for each of the four years I have worked for you, so I could file for my accumulated Earned Income Tax Credits." She give me the damn "uppity Negro" look.

"This is not a back-dated arrangement. The paperwork will be submitted as though I'm hiring you for the first time."

"You are not hiring me for the first time. Before we could open any new book, we must first put the old book in order. I want W-2s to file my past tax returns. If we are going to start applying for tax breaks and filing new papers, this is the way it has to be," I said.

I started walking out the park certain that when she called me back all talk about paperwork would be forgotten. If I insisted on filing old W-2s, the IRS would hold her in a vise grip for life. IRS to white folks was like the INS to illegals.

"Look, Valdi, maybe we will revisit this Earned Income Tax Credit and W-2 discussion at some point," she called after me. We both knew she would never bring that up again. "But, at this moment, what is important is my son. Come back to work, under the old arrangement at the higher salary."

"Seven-fifty."

The fight gone from her voice. "I'll expect you tomorrow."

"Wednesday."

It was only then that she revealed that she had moved into a brownstone far up the West Side. Far enough for it to be called Harlem. Far enough that if I spit it would land in the damn Bronx. I asked what she was doing quite there. She said she had leased the place from a friend with an option to buy and, if the area proved as safe as people in the know were claiming, she would ink a permanent deal.

I didn't want to be ferrying this boy around them judgmental black Harlemites who would perceive my efforts at making a living as prancing on the graves of Martin and Malcolm; kicking Rosa off the bus; canceling the Thirteenth, Fourteenth and Fifteenth Amendments and pissing on the Voting Rights Act. But, again, it was about a rock and a hard place. Was sink or swim.

"Lil fella, talk to me, please!"

I had been begging for an hour, but Cole wouldn't so much as twitch in my direction. I remembered how he would buss out in laughter whenever I scratched "the sweet spot." So I did that ... to no avail.

I sat by the window and read papers for two hours, hoping to bore him out his coma. Still nothing. I got under the sheets and snuggled like when he was little and his folks worked late. He smelt like stale poop. His mother had obviously lapsed back into her self-described, European bathing habits: bathe today, skip, skip, skip, and then bathe day four.

I had drifted off to sleep when his hand finally touched my waist. First, I petted him, and then I marched him to the bathroom. When his dirty pajamas dropped to the floor, he was pure skin and bones. I left the tub to fill up and went to fix him something to eat after his bath. There was only one thing in the fridge: five, crisp, twenty-dollar notes wrapped up in a yellow sticky with "BF" scrawled on it. That meant buy food, which made me panic because this was not the East Side where the boy and I would look normal among the other black babysitter/white child configurations strolling around Fresh Fare. This was Harlem where a situation such as ours would appear counter-revolutionary. But he had to eat. I called Fresh Fare and asked whether there was a good grocery that would deliver to Harlem. The clerk told me that Fresh Fare now had delivery service to Harlem. I was glad for gentrification.

I rattled off my grocery list, as I leaned over the bathtub and gave the boy a good scrubbing. He had to be really sick because, in the old days, there was no way he would just stand there and let me handle him so. He would have sent the phone flying into the tub with one irate swing of his arm.

During the morning, the only thing the boy had said to me was that he missed his dad. I felt badly that the father had not contacted him since he spilt with his mom. At least that's what the mother had told me. But, then, who knows? Maybe she planted that in my head in case her big *sawatee* lawyer called me to testify. If she feel that I would go to court and regurgitate what she had said, she had something else coming to her. I don't enter no government building — municipal, state or federal — and that especially includes courthouses. As the old people used to say, "Aye, I doh have no court-house clothes."

Even if the father was too lost in the squirts of young vaginal juice to remember he had a son right now, I know the day might come when he would show up and claim the boy, as deadbeats eventually do. That's if there was any boy left to claim.

The boy's new personality was a challenge. It was like starting a new work with an entirely new child. He found new ways to piss me off; he was just passive about it.

After I let the water out the tub, instead of climbing out, he laid down in it until I lifted him out. I dropped him on the bed and went in search of a towel. Since the woman had literally squeezed by me as I entered the door that morning without showing me where to find stuff, I was basically on my own. I wiped the boy with the bed sheet and went down to the basement to look for clothes.

At the bottom of the stairs, I pushed open an oak door that creaked like Madam Lucian's kneecaps. Six more steps brought me into a large empty room with four framed photographs on the floor. I picked up the first one, but I couldn't make out anything through the dust that stuck like molasses to the glass. I used my head tie to nudge the gook aside. A thick, brown-skinned woman in a pinched waist-frock and pillbox hat, sitting on the stoop of this very brownstone, looked back at me. Her frozen gaiety suggested she had been instructed to stay very still as the photographer twiddled and fiddled with a box camera under a focusing cloth.

Another photograph, which was also taken in front the brownstone, featured a little man in a Sunday morning suit-coat with a cigar clasped between his thumb and index fingers. The third photograph featured two little girls in three-quarter dresses and shoes and socks playing a handclapping game. In the final photograph, the woman from the first picture was playing a grand piano for three children in this very basement room.

From the way they were dressed, I figured the house once belonged to a 1920s Negro family. Probably not ordinary black folk, but members of that breed of writers, musicians, actors, poets, singers, dancers and thinkers who sewed ideas together to make a giant quilt called "the Harlem Renaissance."

The boy's clothes forgotten, I took the pictures back upstairs with me to the kitchen and perched them on the table. I felt a surge of pride that this home and Harlem had been built, owned and inhabited by people who looked like me. But, even as race pride lifted my chin, I had a niggling sense that a part of the story was missing: a big piece that was incongruous to the idea of well-dressed black families, in a picturesque brownstones, in white, picket-fence-enclosed Harlem.

The *niggler* followed me as I held the cast iron railing that snaked through the brownstone's four floors, still looking for the boy's clothes. It was a certain unsolicited something that drummed in me as I grabbed darts of light thrown by the stain-glass sunroof. It raged unrestrained when I encountered an aquarium in the living room that took up the length and height of the living room wall: a grand microcosm of the sea with thousands upon thousands of snaking vines and grizzly water geezers in colors I had never seen.

I wondered which jazz player had strummed so high, which poet had coined so sweetly to account for such an expansive reward, and so close to the end of the enslavement of African people. Unease pounded as I planted my backside on the same piano bench from the photograph that was now serving as a plant stand in the kitchen. Then it hit me! It hit me hard as the niggler burst blindingly into comprehension. Negroes had not created Harlem from the ground up! White people had to have been here in Harlem before the population shifted and became the pride of black folk, because these elegant brownstones were too nice to have ever been intended for niggers. So white folks moving back into the area was, in essence, chickens coming back home to roost.

They were simply reclaiming what was theirs, and some African-Americans had made it easy by renting for years without buying. While the more ambitious had bought their homes, some had refused to give Caesar his dues. Still, there were those who did everything right, by proudly bequeathing a legacy to their children. Some offspring of that ambitious generation had let that hard work and sacrifice slide into a dump heap. These crack head descendants lounged glass-eyed on stoops, puffing the whole Renaissance away in a haze of acrid smoke, and extinguishing hard-won ideals with penny-liquor-from-a-brown-paper-bag. Harlem ...! African-Americans destroying the legacy of Harlem Negroes.

I swung open the front door of the brownstone and accepted the groceries. As I unpacked the boxes, the woman in the photograph watched with a frozen smile that seemed to carry more than a hint of contempt. I wondered if the hard-won gains she had made were made only in principle because here I was. The gray curtain hovered as I contemplated the yawning void between principle and substance that seemed, like an avaricious *soucouyant,* to slide through the cracks and crevices of the lives of descendants of Africans everywhere in the Diaspora and suck them dry of their hopes, dreams and pride.

My shoulder throbbed. Acknowledging the physical consequences of all this reflection, I turned down the photograph and went to find clothes for the boy.

THE BOY'S PSYCHIATRIST WANTED to see the three of us together. The woman insisted on taking public transportation to get there, forcing me to shuffle alongside them on streets named Malcolm X and Adam Clayton Powell Jr.

In the three weeks since I had started working in Harlem, it was the first time I had even ventured out the front door with the boy. Instead, I had insisted on bringing in a landscaper to fix up the back yard because it had more than enough fresh air for him to breathe back there.

I kept my head straight like I wasn't with them and kept about ten feet ahead. When they caught up, I dropped ten feet behind. It wasn't lost on me that the woman had waited until I was around to *cut her teeth* on the streets of Harlem. Every other day a hired car would pick her up in the morning and drop her off in the evening but, suddenly, she wanted to take the train and the crosstown bus. As I walked along these streets where black women should be walking with black children, I felt like a kidnapped African whose captor gripped my right shoulder with fiery tongs.

My creeping paranoia made me recoil from the toothless women in their thirties who sat on crumbling stoops, their blank stares fixed and rebuking. Men in ancient pimp suits would not move from the middle of the sidewalk, forcing me to deal with them. Young boys with their pants belted beneath their backsides nudged their cohorts as I passed. I make my face say "beast" like I don't care what they think, sloughing through, and praying for an end to this journey.

I did not know when the woman and the boy disappeared, but when I arrived at the train station I couldn't find them. At first, I waited. When they did not come, I retraced my steps. The last time I had been aware of their footsteps behind me, we were around Three Crosses, a nasty looking bodega. I know she wouldn't go in there. So I walked a bit further to see if she had doubled back to the pharmacy on Adam Clayton Powell Jr. Blvd., because everything between the bodega and the subway was being reconfigured to the likings of the population-in-waiting.

I dipped into a few places before returning to the bodega, where I tried peeping into the plexiglas front that was dotted with congealed spit and calcified chewing gum. I took a paper towel from my pocketbook and pushed the door handle. A grimy wood counter took up the entire front of the store. The cashier's appearance alone would have made the woman back out the door. He was swathed in a plush carpet of body hair that practically covered his two bulging eyes. Another worker toiled on a foot-long sandwich, the sweat on his brow seasoning another man's bread. Yet, black folks stood patiently in the line-up waiting to order sandwiches.

The boy stood between the sandwich line-up and the counter as his eyes flirted with thickly iced honey buns, deep-fried pork rinds, candy cigarettes and other ghetto treats he had never seen before. Halfway down the center aisle, the woman was looking at a shelf with dog food, beans, bleach and baby formula.

I shifted my eyes from one to the other, hoping to signal them out. I had just made up my mind to step inside and fetch them when a screech erupted from an androgynous stick with open sores. A dirty slip dress suggested female, despite the thriving moustache. I did a head-to-toe sweep and, to my amazement, saw a dazzling pair of t-strap, silver shoes. A cigarette balancing between lip lines didn't muffle a statement into her cell phone that made my toe curl.

"A white muthafucka be steppin' mah foot and the fucking babysitter didn't say nuttin'."

I didn't have to see the boy's face to know that he was the specific "white muthafucka" in question. He couldn't even breathe when the crack head bent down and blew in his face, bathing him with spit as she berated him for stepping on "Ferragamos dat cost 3Gs." The mother was whimpering in the aisle, desperately trying to get my attention.

"What should I do?" she mouthed like I must know what to do in a case like this.

"Come, boy." I say calmly.

He sparked to life, *faked out* the crack head and lunged behind my back. The crack head stepped into my space, blocking the center aisle just as the woman started her own dash. I gave the woman an eyebrow twitch, and to my surprise she read me. She ran down the center aisle to the back and ran up the first aisle flanked by an *everlasting* beer fridge on one side.

The woman ran past the counter, and straight out the front door without even a glance at the boy, never mind me. The crack head took two giant steps forward, and I make three with the boy attached like a tick to my backside.

The crack head pushed a finger in my face and growled, "Why the fuck you ain't teach dat white boy he better not be stepping on folks' Ferragamos?"

"I didn't know he stepped on your shoes," I said softly.

"Well, now yah know. So whaddayah gonna do about it, niggah?" she say softly, too.

The deli man had a Kaiser roll suspended in midair. Nobody took a breath as they waited to see what I was going to do about it.

"Bitch, ah say whaddayah gonna do 'bout dat white boy be stepping on my Ferragamos?"

"Nothing," I said very, very quietly, and then I thundered, "'Cause I doh like yuh stinking attitude!"

As a confused frown double creased the crack head's brow, I threw myself backward out the door.

"Oh my God! Oh my God! What did I do? I just wanted to be a regular part of the neighborhood, Valdi. I'm so terribly sorry. Thank you, thank you!"

She picked a time like that to cry. I said, "Come on, we don't have time for that. Walk fast!"

The crack head came outside screaming bad words that made even cuss veterans like the woman and me cringe. I kept walking, totally dismissing the crack head. Then she step them Ferragamos on forbidden territory.

"You fuckin' West Indian, cane-picking niggah! If ya want to be babysitting them white muthafuckas, you best be learning how to do it right!"

I stopped dead in my tracks. I spun right around and make a few steps, closing the distance between we. I was about to call she a cotton-picking niggah, a crack head ho and show she exactly where she could stick she crack pipe, but the woman's hand pressing urgently on mine reminded me of who I was in America.

CHANGES

The encounter with the crack head apparently taught the woman to trust me, meaning: for four years she had left her son in my care daily, not knowing if she would ever see him again.

She said things like, "I know you will keep him safe and always put his needs first.

"This is not a job to you, you really care about us.

"Asking you back to work for me was difficult after what happened, but I'm over it now and I know you are too. Let's just say we both took one for the team."

She decided that I was worthy of knowing, so she pestered me for information on my affairs, sometimes lingering whole morning looking for talk. I couldn't even run off with the boy because it would mean walking the streets of Harlem with him.

The woman's work ethic went through the window. Sometimes, in the middle of the day, she would come home to hang with us in the backyard. If I was working in the kitchen, she pulled up a chair there.

She came at me with questions upon questions usually prefaced by, "Valdi, isn't it funny that after all this time we barely know each other?"

I wouldn't find it funny if it were my child involved.

Her idea of building intimacy was to ply me with a spate of questions: Do I enjoy doing childcare? Where have I traveled? Do I want children? Have I ever set goals? Why did I choose America? How did I meet Ava? Did I ever come close to dying? Why did I leave my island? What year was I born? Did I attend college? Have I ever been married? Do I live with anyone? Did I ever lose someone I loved? What was my worst subject in school? Are my parents alive? Do I have siblings?

Through the questioning, I either *skinned and grinned* or was downright rude. But she persisted, evoking unspoken answers that would haunt me all the way to Brooklyn.

This foray into the personal brought us dangerously close to the line between this and that. I found myself doing little extras, like fixing meals for her, too. One morning, after she had eaten a big bowl of cornmeal porridge and belched, she touched me deep inside when she said that I made her house feel like home. She thanked me for the improvements in the boy and, once again, she brought up that stupid crack head.

"Valdi, you did not have to get involved, but you did. You acted when I was paralyzed. I want to do something nice for you. Yo, you got my back, girlfriend."

We both laughed at how stupid she sounded talking that street shit. I could tell that she was really grateful, and I had to busy myself in the pantry so I wouldn't get caught up in her moments. People never really said "thanks" to me, especially not Ava whom I had helped to reach someplace. It was becoming harder to shake off the woman.

The day she belched the cornmeal porridge, she leaned on the counter by the dishwasher and said, "Valdi, there must be something you want ... people, place, animal or thing. Name it, it's yours."

"Place."

"Oooh! Now we're getting somewhere! Where do you want to go?"

"Away from Harlem," I said.

"Not that again. Stop being so dramatic; in a few months the 'delicatessen' (she made quotes with her fingers) would be swallowed by development. I have spoken to some people; don't even worry about it. Seriously, I want to do something extra for you. Of course, you'll always have a job here even after Cole starts school full time. This house needs a lot of care, and perhaps I can throw in some paperwork. You're smart enough for that. What do you think I can do to make you happy?"

I was thinking that I wasn't taking that shit today. So I told her that I was going to dress the boy and take a taxi over to Sherman.

"Well, do you intend to make a career out of this?"

"We will cross that bridge some other time. But, at this moment, I'm going to dress him. I am going to catch up with Ava and the others. It's been a while since he played with his friends."

"Great, I have been meaning to ask you about that. Is your relationship with your friends strained in some way?"

"Everything is fine."

For a moment it looked like she wanted to get dress and come with us, too. I wasn't having that. So, I pointed to the clock. She pushed her chair out hastily.

"Is that really the time? God, I am really enjoying this house and the company. Great porridge, Valdi. Thank you!"

No more than five minutes later she was back in the kitchen, this time holding a stunning powder blue gown.

"Valdi, this is for you. It's an Oscar de la Renta sample I had sent over in your size."

"Blue makes me look fat."

"How about socks? I have a drawer full of new silk ones."

"Silk too itchy."

"Take some juice cartons home with you tonight. I bought extra, just in case."

"It have juice in friggin' Brooklyn," I muttered.

"Did you say something?"

"I said that I'm only drinking water these days."

"I got it," she said excitedly. "I have something very special for you where 'no' will not be an option. I'll be right back."

With that she disappeared into the basement, clacked down the four extra steps and pushed the creaky door open. She practically ran back up the stairs carrying a small silver box that she tenderly placed on the kitchen table. I peeped over her shoulder as she gingerly opened the top to reveal several layers of crinkled black tissue.

"There's a lot of paper in here," she said dejectedly. "It's smaller than I thought."

"What's that?"

"Heaven! Please pass me great-grandmother's silver knife."

I went to the cabinet with the antiques and got the knife. She parted the tissue very, very carefully.

"What is that?"

"Caciocavallo Podolico."

"Cacawho?"

"The most blissful sensation in the world. To think that most will die without this experience. But, not you, Valdi. You are very, very fortunate, because I love you."

A familiar scent hit my nose. "Smell like cheese to me," I said.

"Cheese? Cheese! This, my dear, is delicately crafted from the world's most advanced bovine, Podolica, found only in the wilds of the Picentinis. I did not plan to touch it without a glass of Pauillac but, for you, I will make an exception."

She put a tiny morsel in her mouth and, between groans, she explained that she had received it as a gift for landing a client on the cover of GQ.

"No one in the office knows that I got this. Now, sit and buckle up for a ride to heaven."

I couldn't believe how stupid she was getting over a piece of cheese. I decided to have a little fun. I ignored the chair she had pulled out for me and strolled over to the pantry where I moved things around on the shelf.

"You're not going to try this?"

"Not now."

"Valdi, are you crazy? Get over here right now."

"Look, I'm not hungry right now. Just cut me a big chunk and wrap it in foil. I will make a pot of mac and cheese when I get home."

I fled down to the basement, sat on the toilet and giggled at the look she gave me at the thought of her good Caciowhatever vanishing in a sea of milk, egg and black pepper.

I never saw or heard about that cheese again.

But that didn't stop her from trying to find other ways to reward me. One day she dropped by Sherman toting a fancy sandwich for my lunch. I felt like she was GPSing me. I took the sandwich to get rid of her fast. Monica grabbed the bag from my hand and went at it like she didn't eat for d-a-y-s. She stopped to lick the mustard cream running down her fingers.

"Lawd, ah what ah nice sandwich dis. Brruuuuuurp! 'Scuse me. Valdi, you mus ah control yuh affairs. Chloë can't come *buck up 'pon* us like dat. We must move to another spot in the park."

"I can't move from here," Madam Lucian say.

We all knew that. She and her brood were the reason we hung out in such an exposed area. At her age, is only so far she could push that so-called stroller.

"That's right; Madam Lucian can't move, so we nah move. So you ah 'ave to 'andle your story. Let Chloë do something nice ah fuh you, so she ah leave you alone. Yuh always have to be rigid. Take something from wan woman and buy everybody some peace."

Ava, who was making a rare appearance at Sherman, said that her boss was welcome anytime. I said nothing, 'cause nothing was all I had to say to Ava these days. A selection from Dittersdorf's *Finale: Prestissimo – Allegretto* (at least that's what Ava say it is) percolated from her cell phone again, grating on my last nerve.

"Hello. Good afternoon," she said in her telephone accent.

Soon Cinderella buss out in radiant smile. I put my head in my newspaper so I could listen in peace. She spoke loudly so I did not have to strain myself. When she was finished, she was laughing and crying at the same time. She say the executive director of the Board of Education was so impressed by her application that he had called personally to offer her a fast-track position in something or the other.

Ava's voice faded as something whizz through my head like the sound of a stone from a slingshot. I had expected Ava to graduate and get a real work one day. I had expected it since the day I had showed her the Medgar Evers College ad and suggested she give it some thought. But that didn't cushion the punch in my gut now that the moment had arrived, because who would have thought that I would have been in exactly the same place? I sat on Sherman steps trying to figure out how I should act when her drone was over. "Congratulations, Ava," would be too pat and painfully insufficient since Monica and Madam Lucian were dancing like two *red bamsee chimpanzee.* I located my feet and wobbled up as the others peppered her with questions.

"Congratulations, Ava. That's nice." I said, pleased that my mouth had found two extra words.

Ava responded, "thank you."

But, by her tone, she might as well have said, "fuck you."

That bitch wanted me to jump up and scream like the others, to make at least two series of cartwheels 'round Sherman's horse before bending over to kiss she royal ass. While the gross ebullience from the others was nice, she wanted to get that from me, too.

"Well, this is the day you been bussing your brains over them books for."

My mouth had spoken again. She offered a half-nod and turned her attention to Monica who was demanding to know all about "Ava big wuk."

"Imagine, ah me, Monica, could tell people my sister work for the Board of Educayshan."

I eased slowly over to the children playing in the grass.

"Who want to play dodge ball?" I asked.

The suspicious looks they give me make me feel bad that I wasn't exactly known as the life of the party. But they crowded me anyway, Cole, Madam Lucian's healthy boy, Ava's twin, Monica's boys, plus some of their little friends. I racked my brain to remember how to play dodge ball or "scooch" as we called it back home. I told the boy that he and I had to hit the others with the ball to get them out. I couldn't help glancing over at Ava and the rest who were still in the moment. I didn't realize how hard I was pelting the ball until a girl screamed out. I let a Yugoslav nanny throw.

The light breeze that had opened the morning had gathered strength. It picked up the ball and blew it all the way to Sherman. Delighted, the children ran against the wind, fighting their way towards the statue to see who could reach it first. Ava and the others looked up at the darkening clouds as they tried to figure out where to take the party next.

Now that she had been offered her dream job, Ava's purpose had ripened just like Madam Lucian's whose house was basically finished. Even Monica had finally received notification of her Green-Card interview. As for me, *I just dey*. I warned that a thunderstorm couldn't be far behind, and say that I had to get the boy home before the rain. Monica took me aside and begged me to come with them to the café at the museum to toast Ava with hot chocolate. She put her fingers to her lips and told me not to say anything about Ava's job in front the twins, as Ava wanted to surprise her employers with the news when the time was right.

What-ever!

I told Monica that Harlem too far for me to play with monsoons, and that the woman had just called to say she needed to speak to me immediately. When I said goodbye, Ava barely answered, and Madam Lucian looked pained. Monica said she hoped that the woman didn't want nothing serious, making me feel bad for lying. As I walked across the plaza with my arm around the boy, I could feel their eyes burning into my back. I knew Madam Lucian and Monica feel that I just jealous of Ava, but that was too simple.

Two yellow taxis pulled in front the brownstone at the same time, one with me and the boy, the other with the woman. My lie proved prophetic cause the woman said, "Valdi, I need to discuss something with you immediately."

She sat me down in the study and asked me if I had enjoyed the sandwich that she had had Chef Marquis prepare especially for me.

"Monica said it was very good," I say.

"Well, at least you're honest."

She said she was hurt to see Monica eating the sandwich but that sparked an epiphany.

"I realized that you have never accepted anything from me except wages, taxi fare and your Christmas bonuses, despite the many gifts I have offered you over the years."

She asked why that was so. I asked why she was spying on me in the park.

"Valdi, it was nothing ... only dodge ball. It's not like you were doing something wrong. Now stop evading my question."

I say some foolishness about how my father taught me not to envy what people have and refusing other people's stuff was part of that. She called that line of reasoning nonsense, and insisted that the time had come to name my reward for handling the crack head so efficiently.

I remember how Monica said that if I let the woman do something for me she would revert to the old boundaries. I agreed to accompany her to dinner to repay the debt, and she set the date for that Friday. She didn't ask if I had plans, but I didn't fuss about that. I did insist, however, that she keep the outing very casual.

Monica called. I told her that I was going to dinner with the woman. It struck me that Monica was the only person whom I talked to outside the working day, the stuff with Ava being what it is. Speaking to Madam Lucian had, of late, turned into a chore because she always found a way to bring every damn topic back to that house.

I gripe with Monica that every time I socialize with these people it turned out badly.

She say, "Valdi, try ah leave dat chip 'pon your shoulder at your 'ouse."

ON FRIDAY NIGHT, I followed the woman out the taxi, which had pulled up in front a tiny, mossy building sandwiched between two towering glass buildings at 79th and 5th. The place looked so rundown I wondered if I had overstated my desire to keep it simple. The woman walked to the side of the building and swiped a card to open a small red door. I hesitated outside, peeping over her shoulder as she stepped in.

"Valdi, come in," she said, yanking me.

Inside looked sacred, like a church with a bar instead of an altar. The golden Aristotle at the front entrance, the streaks of stain glass running down the walls, and the overall Gothic theme of the room all seemed vaguely familiar. When I asked the woman where we were, she just smiled. Then it dawned on me that I was in the legendary O.L., a supper club and workspace for writers that I had seen pictures of in an architectural journal at somebody's house.

"Is this the Order of Letters Club?" I asked the woman.

Incredulity was too simple a word to describe how she looked at me. It was as if my question had stripped her naked and she was scrambling to position one arm across her breasts and another on her vagina.

"Valdi, who are you really? How could you possibly know that?"

I felt really, really naked, too. I asked her why she had brought me here.

"You came to my reception at The Winsford to see the writers. Well, here you are Valdi ... writers. Be careful, they are usually drunk."

She disappeared for a moment and returned carrying two jeweled pins with curly letters saying Order of Letters.

"Emeralds and diamonds. Honor system. We return them when we leave," she said, attaching one to me.

Hers looked like mine except for a check mark that probably differentiated members from guests. She led me to the tuxedo-clad host, a handsome, silver-haired man who greeted her by name and asked whether she was meeting someone.

"I'm here with someone, now," she said.

"Together?" He did not look at me at all.

"Isn't it obvious?" Her voice had taken on a low, guttural tone that I had never heard before.

"Actually, Madam, it isn't," he said.

"Had I been standing here with a white woman would you have said, 'together?'" Her voice was rising. I squeezed her arm.

"It's okay," I whispered.

"First, you will apologize, and then you will lead us to your best table for two."

"I apologize," he said staring only at the woman and when she stabbed him with her eyes, he turned to me and said it too. And in that instant Chloë became more than a pay check.

The crack head had turned the gulf between us to mud, and now a waiter had hardened it. As writers stopped by the table to pay homage, she introduced me as "my friend, Valdi." Though the statement wouldn't fit in real life if the woman and I had encountered the same folks on the street and the boy were there; tonight it was okay. She even took care of questions thrown at me by a black woman writer who inquired about my book titles. The woman told her that I wrote in French.

"I hope you didn't mind, Valdi. It seemed simpler."

I tapped the menu. An unusual night deserved some unusual fare. I decided on turtle soup and alligator filet with white truffle mushrooms. The woman took a long time to decide, as her palate had become jaded with familiarity. I instructed her to eat a hamburger and fries, and she said it was years since she had had that. We washed down our dinner with a few cocktails, and she got to tool around a bit in my private life. I proffered an abridged version about my Columbia experience. She said that my personality didn't fit with writing. I said that babysitting had boiled the personality out of me.

"Were you any good?" she asked.

I told her that I wasn't sure, because it was a long time ago. She said that, given her line of work, we could have met under completely different circumstances. She placed her hand on mine. I tried to wiggle free, but she held on.

"Valdi, look at me. No, look here."

Her eyes were bleary and pained. She was squeezing my fingers so tightly, my graduation ring pushed deep into my flesh.

"Faaaldi." She slurred my name like she was tasting it for the first time. "I am sorry that you didn't hear the writers that night."

"I'm seeing them tonight," I said, rubbing her hand lightly as I rescued mine.

More cocktails; a shared desert. We left the supper club hand in hand giggling and trying to focus on walking a straight line. I waited in the shadows as she hailed two cabs. The lucky one headed to the Upper East Side; the other to Brooklyn. And as the taxi cruised over the Brooklyn Bridge, I reflected on the thawing between us. If we had inhabited the same stratosphere, we really could have been friends. I recalled the intimate details she had confided about her life and marriage; stuff I would no longer tell the girls.

ALL FALL DOWN

The more the boy's health improved, the less he wanted to stay home, which was bad business for me considering Ava's crap. He kept begging to go back by Sherman, which I was avoiding. So I suggested that we arrange some play dates with new friends, but he was not buying that, and start harassing me from morning 'til night.

"What's wrong with my old friends?

"Why don't you come to pick me up from school at the same time as Ava picks up my friends?"

Why this, and how come that?

Lawd!

One afternoon, I swear he nagged me out the door and into a taxi heading to Sherman. I found the three of them so wrap up in their discussion about Ava's graduation party that they didn't even see me until I was nearly on top of them. Ava saw me first and *ginch* like she get ketch thiefing something. Monica and Madam Lucian looked sheepish and, quick time, the conversation done. For the boy's sake, I wanted to make everybody comfortable and show I had no hard feelings, so I crack a little joke to fill the silence.

"Aye, Ava gyrl, I come for my graduation ticket."

I shoulda keep my damn mouth shut. Ava mumbled about only having three tickets.

So Monica say, "Dat 'nuff. Ah jus' three of us. Ava, don't say yuh ah give tickets to your boss and not to us?"

Monica looked like she was going to cry.

"Ava, maybe your people would agree to sit this one out if they knew how badly your friends wanted to go," I said, trying to sound light and non-confrontational.

"There would have been no graduation ceremony or party without them," Ava say with an edge to her voice.

"Why? Did they go to school and study for you?" I ask, my voice dripping molasses.

"The real question is: Why does discord reign as soon as you make an appearance?" Ava replies, getting pompous.

"Alright, alright," Monica say. "We ah go crash the ceremony. To besides, we will still 'ave wan good time at Ava's party, nuh so? Let's talk about the clothes we goin' wear."

Ava collected the twins and flew out the park. Monica and Madam Lucian didn't say much to me after that, and I feel as though they blamed me for mashing up the lime. The boy wasn't ready to leave, so I left the two sourpuss on Sherman steps and joined the boy on the grass. I organized the second ballgame of my babysitting life: a soccer game with boys versus girls. At least the boy was happy with me.

He say, "Valdi, you are the best babysitter ever."

I took the helm of the girls' team, and another parent volunteered to coach the boys. In no time, parents and babysitters got into the game, with one parent pledging water ices for the victors and another promising to buy for the vanquished. I asked the boys' coach to make Cole captain of the team and the goalie.

"He needs a little boost of confidence. Don't worry he can score goals."

Just after half time I realized that the ball was no longer in play. I squinted up the field and saw Cole with the ball in his hand talking to a man. I watched for a couple minutes and, when it did not seem to be breaking up, I raced up the field and found the boy with his heart on the ground. The man was his asshole father, and he was with his Russian slut of a baby-sitter. I took the ball from the boy and threw it back into the game.

"Are you okay, lil fella?" I asked.

He didn't have to look up for me to see tears carving a dirt road in his face.

"It's okay. We don't have to stay. Tell your Dad goodbye."

"Good game," the asshole say to me. "Valdi, upon reflection, it is the first time I have ever seen you off your fat ass."

"Well, upon reflection, it's the first time I have ever seen you with so much hair. Is it a toupée or hair plugs?"

The girl laughed and rubbed the boy's neck. He squirmed away. She did it again.

"He does *not* like that," I said coldly.

The asshole told the boy that he was leaving and ruffled his hair. The boy flung his arms around his father's waist and clung like a limpet. Impatiently, the girl inserted her fingers between the asshole's shirt buttons, lifted her chin to him and pouted her lips. He responded, and the tenuous moment he was having with his son evaporated. The boy raced off toward the statue bawling his eyes out. I turned to follow him but, first, I *sipped a little bush tea for Cole's fever.*

"How dare you? You have no damn shame! Look what you did to your little boy?" I fumed.

He looked surprised to see that the boy was no longer there.
"No, how dare *you!?*" His face grew florid.

"You are nothing but a fucking nigger, and I've been waiting for four years to call you that!"

"And you're nothing but a nasty asshole!" I spat in his face.

I felt no satisfaction, for "asshole" could never neutralize the power of "nigger." As I left, he fired his parting salvo.

"You'll regret this! When I'm finished with you, you won't get hired to watch even a *bedbug* in New York City."

We turned in opposite directions and, when I almost reach Sherman, Monica came speeding over to me.

"Valdi, what 'appen? Me had to sit 'pon the bwoy to stop 'im 'ead from banging 'pon the concrete. Him ah pee inna him pants."

I found three babysitters restraining the boy as he screamed himself into fits. I dialed 911, and then I called the woman and told her what happened. She said to have the ambulance take him to Lenox Hill Hospital and she would meet me there. I told her to hurry up. A lump was rising on his forehead, and I didn't want to walk in that hospital without the woman to a whole heap of questions about how he get that. I wish Ava was there to go with him in the ambulance. I check for my Columbia ID, in case I had to show something.

I experience one moment of mercy 'cause the ambulance and a taxi bearing the woman pulled into the hospital's emergency entrance at the same time. She took the boy's insurance card from me and went in with him to triage. She didn't emerge for hours, and when she did, she was surprised to see me there still. I waited with her overnight through the boy's evaluations and scans.

Doctors said the bump would go away, but the boy had some deeper issues. Their diagnosis was Affective Mood Disorder, with a possibility of Bipolar Disorder. The latest episode with his father had shut him down so completely that he stopped responding to people. He stayed in hospital for five days and came home not much improved. He displayed only occasional flashes of his former self.

He had seven different pills to take. He wouldn't eat, so he had to take a pill for that. He didn't sleep, so he had a pill for that. He was depressed so he had two pills for that. The area around the bump was still sensitive, so he had something for that too, and on and on it went. When Ava, Monica and Madam Lucian brought the children to play, he just lay there watching them. It did not have no pill to make him play.

I start to have my own little episodes. My shoulder started back. I would be in an air-conditioned room and my body would just spring water. And the voice keep whispering all the time.

Move on, the situation getting too complicated. Lawyers talking about subpoenas, affivadits, and notaries!

The voice like smoke soon became a raging chorus with each one vying for supremacy.

Move on! Get out, now! They are planning to sue you for the boy's condition!

You will have to go to court and testify against the boy father!

Trinidad waiting for you!

You are going to make a real maco man of your father now! Ha ya yie!

It was also physically draining. Half the time, the boy refused to walk and I had to lift him, which created a lancing pain in my lower back. The whole situation was a big emotional tax. The woman had nobody; her parents resided in an assisted-living community in Florida, and her two sisters were estranged. So, to ease the pressure, we take to sipping brandy at night, while she gave me some real insight into life on the other side. She say that she is a "Manhattan and Hyde Park Van Buren who had picked a husband from a Maricopa trailer park."

Like many other nights, she drifted off after she had reached her limit, but I had learned to hold my liquor, and so I kept my ears open to listen for the boy. Soon, whether we *take a taste* or not, the whole weight of night nursing became my sole responsibility. The woman went back to her career in the outside world; mine became the boy's well-being.

For my own sanity, I searched my brain for a way to woo the boy back from the unknown refuge into which he had retreated. I called Ava and, like me, she was convinced that Cole was grieving over the loss of his father. I tried to convince the woman to forget the court judgment and let the boy see him. She explained exactly how many icebergs would have to thaw in a frozen hell before she would allow that to happen. I made the same suggestion to Cole's psychiatrist, but she said an encounter with the father was too big a risk to take. I disagreed. She knew medicine, true, but I believe that sometimes we must return to the beginning in order to change the ending. To me, the woman and the doctor were doing nothing but sedating the fire out the boy. He was like a rag doll: anywhere you put him, he stayed. I had the feeling that if I placed him in a tub of water, he would just lie there and drown.

I told the woman to take him back to the hospital for a second opinion, but she worried that he would be institutionalized. When I tell her that the responsibility was too much and gave notice, she gave me a raise, which was the only good thing in this whole situation. My savings were growing nicely, 'cause I had no time to spend any of it.

I did have a support system of sorts. Ava dropped by and phoned a few times, although she made it clear she was only interested in the boy. Madam Lucian visited once to show me she people new baby. My heart hurt for her. She now had four children to see 'bout, three of whom still used a stroller. The baby added exactly ten dollars a week to her paycheck. I teasingly asked if her boss had added a second floor to the stroller. On the serious side, I advised Madam Lucian to quit the hustle and focus on her bread business. She said that they missed me on Friday nights.

"Remember, Valdi, one bread, one brick goes for you too."

Monica really propped me up. She visited almost every day to catch me up on the goings on around Sherman and the rumors on the nannyvine. She also called nightly at nine. I looked forward to her calls because her spirit was so light, and her jokes so amusing, that my spirit expanded beyond the confines of the boy's room. Monica was troubled by the coldness between Ava and me, and asked how she could help mend the fence. I told her that it had wounded me deeply that Ava feels that I not happy to see her make it, and she should know better after all the help I gave her with her essays.

"Lawd-mi-done! Valdi ah you ah 'elp Ava with essay?" Monica was shocked. "Me ah forget you ah went college, you nah mention it much. Ah truth you nah regular like me."

I told her that I had graduated from the University of the West Indies at the top of my class and had rejected a government scholarship to pursue post-graduate studies in the Caribbean in favor of an oil company's offer to study abroad.

"When I lost my scholarship, I had to drop out. I owed money that I couldn't repay let alone find additional fees."

"Gyrlfriend, did you ask *Dan Dadda* in your school to ah 'elp yuh?"

"The available grants were for American students. Anyway, nobody was listening to a foreigner owing thirty Gs."

"Dat ah only chump change for Dan Dadda. Valdi, you 'ave to learn to ask for what you want."

Monica say that Columbia isn't the only school in America, and ask why I didn't go to Medgar Evers College like Ava.

"'Is wan cheap school, nuh so?"

"Medgar does not have a postgraduate program," I tell Monica.

"Is college, nuh so?"

"Yes, but Ava was studying for a bachelor's degree. I did that at UWI already. I was working on my Masters at Columbia."

Monica say it sounded like the same thing to her.

"Okay, Monica, the level that Ava just finished, I completed that twenty years ago at UWI."

"So dats 'ow you could write essays for Ava," Monica said.

"It was no big deal, Monica. I just helped her out of a jam now and then. So how are things with you?"

"Chuh! If you 'elp Ava with school, it not right that she tell Madam Lucian and me ah 'ow you jealous."

Monica said it so casually like she didn't just release a bomb. Just as casually, I said goodnight.

The next night the phone rang as I lay on the cot reading. I picked it up, prepared to tell Monica that I was sleeping and would talk to her some other time. It was Ava. She called to cuss me out for the "damn lies" I had told Monica. I look at the clock; it was after ten. Monica had not called.

"Valdi, did you tell Monica that you wrote all my essays?"

"I don't know what she said, but it sounds out of context."

"What was the context? Did you say that you wished you had had the opportunity to write essays for Ava?"

"Ava, stop. You know how Monica is."

"She couldn't make this up without help from you. So tell me about this essay you supposedly wrote for me. All I had ever asked you to do is cast your eye on my papers."

Ava was acting like I did no more than identify an errant comma. Look like she forget that I had spent years performing surgery on her sentence fragments, run-ons, comma splices, mixed constructions, faulty parallelisms, dangling participles and week voice.

"You have to give me a little more credit than that."

"Whatever for?"

"For distinguishing between *sophia* and *phronesis* when you were stuck. For exploring how practical wisdom straddles and mediates between moral and intellectual virtues. That was the thirty-page, A+ paper on Aristotle that I wrote for you, the time you dropped seventeen books on my ex-boss' kitchen table and turned your back."

"I gave you one hundred and thirty dollars for that."

"That does not erase the fact that I wrote the paper."

Ava say that reproach is the lowest quality to be found in a human being, and that I must never darken her doorway ever again.

"It's not that serious Ava, I was just making a point."

I know that my tone sounded like begging, but I didn't want us to end like that because, in my heart, I was happy for Ava. I only wanted to stay relevant. I was about to tell her that when she give me the dial tone. I kept calling Monica all night to cuss she out, but she smell the rat; she did not answer.

When the woman woke up, I told her she had to stay home because I had things to do.

I ARRIVED BY Sherman about one o'clock, but only Madam Lucian was there. She cradled the new baby on her bosom, while the toddler and the sickly one slept in the stroller. She said the other boy had gone with his parents to elementary school interviews. I asked her for Monica and Ava. She said that Monica did not come to work, and she had not heard from Ava.

"Madam Lucian, did you hear about the confusion that Monica made between Ava and me?" I asked.

"Valdi, I telling you like I told Monica last night. Don't get me involved. You all wasting life on nonsense. I can't take it. I have enough problems on my plate."

I looked at Madam Lucian, I mean really looked at her, because it was the first time I had had ever heard the word problem come out her mouth. I put my arm around her.

"Lucie girl, wha wrong wid you today?"

To my chagrin, waves and waves of tears spurted out happy-go-lucky Madam Lucian's eyes and cascaded down her cheeks. I tried to console her, but it was like trying to cork the sea. She staggered to her feet, and I had to catch the people infant that came rolling off her lap.

"Madam Lucian, what is it? What has happened to you?"

My mind jumped from cancer to deportation to job loss. Her hand vibrated as she grabbed hold of the crucifix dangling from a chain around her neck.

"Madam Lucian?"

"Oh Valdi," she wept, her ample bosom convulsing. "There is no house!"

"There is no house," Madam Lucian said again, her voice crack-ing under the weight of a crushing finality.

The infinite bigness of that sentence sent me reeling back to the first day I met Madam Lucian — back when I was working for the woman with the twin girls. It was the second Friday in the month. Of this, I am certain, not because meeting Madam Lucian was such a cataclysmic event, but because, back then, the second Friday of the month was the only day that Ava and I were not together. On this day, she usually had a set play date with a family that owned a dog.

So, like all other second Fridays, was just me alone pushing my stroller through Central Park. I was taking my time going down-hill when what seemed like a flash of light danced up ahead. It caught the girls' eyes too, because they sat up in the double stroller and clapped and cooed. The light bobbed up, down, right, left. I walked quickly toward it, and found a thick mane of silvery-gray hair, whose splendor suggested it deserved to be on a pedigree horse. I had never seen hair like that. So I barreled past the middle-aged woman who pushed a contraption that looked like it had started out as a stroller, but had morphed into this perplexing monstrosity.

I sat on a park bench to watch her approach. She walked with a slight limp as she toted a baby strapped on her chest. The stroller contained another child, while a small boy walked alongside. Her relaxed and pleasant countenance made me wonder what the hell was so good about watching three children at her age. A cloud descended. For a split second, I had the strange and uncomfortable sensation that I was actually watching myself approaching me in twenty years' time.

As she drew close to the bench, I said, "Excuse me, Ma'am, how do you handle seeing 'bout all those children?"

"I have more vigor than you," she said, coating me with a stream of sonorous sounds that chased my melancholy away.

"You right, 'cause I couldn't make myself do that," I said.

"Baby, you have to do what you need to do. Young girl like you saying 'can't,'" she reproached me while leaning breathlessly on her stroller.

"I didn't say 'can't,' I said 'couldn't.' Come sit here and rest a while."

She told the boy that he could play in the grass, and detached the squirming infant from the carrier. She eased on to the bench and leaned over to whisper softly to a tiny boy in the stroller who looked like a little old man. She said that the baby was six months old, the boy tooling around was three, and the little old man in the stroller was nine but, when he was a baby, he had had a tumor that retarded his growth. The baby kept pulling on her beautiful mane.

"Why don't you put the baby in the stroller so you can relax?" I said, pointing to the empty space. She explained that the disabled boy attacks the baby.

"I can only put the baby in there when he sleep," she said.

She pulled a home décor magazine from beneath the stroller and fanned herself vigorously.

"Mon dieu, it hot."

"Where you from?" I asked.

"Sent Lisi, West Indies," she say. Catching the confusion on my face she laughed, "Fancy name for St. Lucia."

"That's why I couldn't put my finger on your accent. You're the first person I have met from the French Caribbean who is not Haitian. I'm Valdi," I said grabbing her hand.

"I am Dorothé," she say embarking on this long story about how folks does always say she name wrong, and how the stress must go a particular place to give the proper sound and that the last syllable have to sound like "thay not tee." I say that is too hard for me, and since she from St. Lucia, I going to call her 'de Lucian.'

"De Lucian? Eh-eh. But, young girl, you too fresh. You cannot call me 'de Lucian'; you must say 'Madam Lucian.'"

With that, she flung her head back and the mane danced to the beat of her chuckles.

"Madam Lucian," she laughed. "I like it. Oui, you can call me Madam Lucian."

I could not take my eyes off that hair. She answered my unspoken question with pride.

"I'm Garifuna. Black Carib, a descendant of the Garinagu Indians who invaded St. Vincent long, long time ago and conquered the Arawaks, and breed with the Africans who get shipwrecked on the island. The British came and start some confusion, and some of my people ended up in St. Lucia. That is the line that I come from."

Madam Lucian was so great a conversationalist that I forgot to miss Ava. We talked about the islands for a while and the conversation naturally moved to babysitting. For the record, Madam Lucian started it.

"So how the work?"

"It alright. I been with these girls since they were four days old. But, really, how do you make out?"

"Well, I only watch the one that running about part of the day, he goes to school in the hotel opposite General Sherman, you know that gold statue on the horse by Columbus circle? I just picked him up and decided to take a little walk up the East Side. This other two I mind all day."

"Why don't you find an easier situation?"

"I working with them since the sick one born. Then I see they come with the one running on the grass. Few months ago they give me this baby. What an old lady going to do?

"I feel bad for you. Do you mind if I ask your age?"

"Ask and you will see."

"How old?"

"Just turned sixty-five," she said.

"And you have to work so hard?"

She thought the pity in my voice was for her, when I was actually feeling sorry for myself in advance. Her tone got a little chilly, and she said that she didn't need my pity as she had a plan. Leaning closer, she glanced around left and right and dropped her voice.

"One bread, one brick," she said.

As I pondered that, she wiggled her fingers into the stroller's inside pocket and pulled out a worn manila envelope. She extracted a frail document from the envelope, which she unfolded over the stroller until the hairy boy couldn't even be seen.

"What's this?"

"This is my house," she said her voice cracking, "This is what I working for."

"You start building yet?"

"Groundbreaking is in one month," she said.

"You like my house?" she asked watching the paper like it already had stucco walls and was sitting on a manicured lawn. I nodded.

"How long you in America?" I asked.

"Ten years."

"I hope you don't find me outta place, but how could you afford it? The people you work for must pay very well."

"I only get three hundred and ten dollars a week for these children."

"Dat is advantage-taking. So how do you make ends meet never mind put aside money to build house?"

"I am the Flatbush Bread Lady," she said proudly.

I knew exactly what she was talking about. The Flatbush Bread Lady was an institution to any Caribbean person who had ever partied late and craved bake and fish at 3:00 a.m., or wanted a fresh loaf on a Saturday morning. I had never been to her apartment personally, but I had waited in a car while a stupid *Bajan* man I was seeing went to buy bread for me and his wife.

"I have tasted your bread; it is delicious," I said.

"Well, chile, that is how I get money to build house. I sell one bread for three dollars and that is able to buy one brick in St. Lucia. I name my plan, 'Bread for Brick.'"

That is how it began with Madam Lucian and me.

I promised to introduce her to my friend, Ava, and she said I would meet her young friend, Monica, the next week. It wasn't until about five Fridays later that I met Monica, because she had gotten fired for taking the girl she was seeing about to an appointment she had with a "masseuse." Her boss had found out when the girl went home and blabbed that Monica had taken off her clothes and a man rubbed her back. It had taken Monica a few weeks to find work in the neighborhood.

As soon as I set eyes on Monica, I knew exactly who she was: Trenchtown's answer to a behind-the-bridge-Trinidad-bad-girl. Plus, Jamaicans always had to add a little ketchup on everything;

so she had the entire look down pat: make-up cake into a scar that travelled from her nose to temple. Her breasts and shirt seemed to be at cross-purposes in the battle for modesty. Her weave updo looked like a bird nest, and she had unbelievably long nails that made me wonder how she wash "down there" without harming herself. Monica was the type that gossiped plenty, deflowered boys, pulled knives, and sowed confusion and discord. She probably had lived bad and hard in Jamaica, and ran to America *when water drowned flour.*

She elbowed me out the way when I tried to change the sickly boy's diaper. In a squeaky voice, she told me that she and Madam Lucian was tight, pressing two fingers together to show me that not even air could pass between them. She said that Madam Lucian had never once charged her "fi she bread." Although it was clearly a warning that Madam Lucian belonged to her, I enjoyed liming with Monica. Her humor was crude: like how she told Madam Lucian that the only thing the architect forgot to draw in the house is a "stiff" man. Through her chuckles, Madam Lucian told Monica that she was too *slack.*

The new lime get so sweet that I relegated Ava to Monday and Wednesdays only when she refused to come and meet the people I was telling her about. Ava did not want to leave the park at E. 72nd, and I couldn't ask Madam Lucian to leave Sherman with that wagonload of children. I continued to press Ava.

"My priority is my children," Ava say. "The area surrounding General Sherman Tecumseh's statue is more courtyard than a playground. How are the children supposed to run and play? It's also too close to the road."

"The children will make out fine. There is grass in an adjoining area," I told Ava.

It was only after I said that General Sherman was a great American soldier to introduce to the children, and that the Museum of Modern Art was just up the block, that she decided to "try it for just one afternoon." After that session, she was hooked. Citing her fondness for "people with ambition," she told Madam Lucian that she would help her run errands for her bread business.

Ava tell Madam Lucian that both of us were going to help her bake on Friday nights without even consulting me. Though that get me mad-vex, I went. So, to hear "there is no house" — after kneading all that dough in that sweltering apartment; poring over home décor magazines and a stained blueprint while four of us sit in a huddle; placing furniture in imaginary rooms; squabbling over the difference between marigold yellow, saffron yellow and dark goldenrod; packing tools in barrels for shipment; and performing countless duties associated with building house and making home — was unthinkable! To understand that statement, I would have to accept that Madam Lucian had kneaded about twenty landfills of flour, and grated through plantations of cassava for nothing. I didn't want to understand what she was feeling. I wanted no part of it.

So when I asked, "what happened?" it was because somebody had to ask, and I was the only one there. I couldn't call Ava because she wasn't talking to me, and I couldn't call Monica because I wasn't talking to her. That left me to bear the burden of this old lady who was bawling out, "there is no house!"

The baby cried, and I was glad to stand up and rock her to avoid Madam Lucian's eyes.

She spoke.

"I am seventy-five years old," she said.

The surprise must have shown in my face because she continued, "When we first met I had just turned seventy-two, I'm sorry that I told you then that I was sixty-five."

After a brief pause, she continued, "I come from the village of Bouton, where my mother grow up fourteen of us; thirteen were girls and the last was the boy child she loved. My father was a hard-working man who grew from child laborer to the paymaster on the sugarcane estates. As the second child, I was one of the few who remembered the day when prosperity came and Papa knocked down the tapir house and built one that was not much bigger, but it was built with bricks.

"Papa went to work in the fields one day and didn't return. Some say jumbie hold him, others say the plow rolled over him. Mami cuss his corpse for leaving her with all these 'damn children.'

"My older sister was sixteen. Before the n*ine-night ceremony* had even come, she run off with a *dadder-head* Grenada boy. That's what Mami call him, and she never referred to them again.

"With the exception of my brother and the three youngest girls, we were taken out of school and sent to work in a neighbor's garden. Since I was now the oldest by default, I was taught to make bread that I sold in the market alongside the produce the neighbor exchanged for labor. I also cooked, cleaned, washed, starched and ironed.

"So when the old, yellow man get fresh in the market and say how he wanted to marrid to me and give me house, I did not mind. I was fifteen and he was nearly fifty. I didn't want to shame myself like my sister, so I tell him if he serious to go and ask my mother for permission and warned him not to go empty-handed. When I reached home that day my mother smiled at me for the first time. She said how I should push my clothes in a paper bag because I have husband now. She had handed me over for two sack-a-flour, a bag of rice, a bag of corn meal, and a cotton handbag.

"That is how I went to live with this man who smell like rum, sweat and cigarette. Though he forced me regularly, no children never come from it. He beat me, he bathe me; he beat me, he bathe me. Early on, I started praying that God take him, but he never went nowhere until he was ninety-eight. He left me penniless at sixty-five, squatting on government land."

Madam Lucian paused and buried her head in her hands as if she were back there in the moment when she came in from Mistah Alcindore's funeral and peered into the cupboard at the one item — salt biscuit.

The sun was setting and its rays fruitlessly caressed Madam Lucian who was shaking like she had ague. The disabled boy was trying to tip the stroller, causing his little sister to wake up with a start. The infant on my lap was sucking hungrily on her finger.

I told Madam Lucian that she had to take the children home, but she couldn't hear me. I wanted to block my ears from that tragic tale. I wanted to un-hear all that she had already said, for with knowledge comes responsibility and I wanted to be responsible only for myself.

Already, I missed the Madam Lucian with the sonorous laughter and deep voice — my friend, the Flatbush Bread Lady, who was building a big house. I didn't want to know Dorothé, who was sold for "two-sack-a-flour." How I could listen to her laugh again, knowing it could not possibly be coming from her gut? Suddenly, I was angry. I had come here solely to cuss out Monica, and Madam Lucian had dumped this shit on me.

"Yuh want water?" I muttered. Is like I didn't say nothing; she kept talking.

"So I sit there eating biscuit when, out of the blue, Boyo came to see me. I hadn't seen him in over thirty years because Mami had put him on a ship at fourteen and sent him England to study. At forty-four, he was rich enough to return to Sent Lisi with his British wife and build a big house. I never use to see him often 'cause he hated Mistah Alcindore but, now that he was dead, my brother had ventured up the hill.

"When he saw my condition he started to cry. 'Doro,' he said. 'Why you didn't tell me?'

"Then I told him it was alright, and that I would get by because I was accustomed. To my surprise he said, 'I will help you. You know you are my favorite sister.'

"He and de wife Pipa made me put on my Sunday best and

they took me for a ride in their car; a new one that smelled like leather. Pipa asked if I wanted to come and live with them, but I refused. My brother asked me what I was going to do now, as if it had something else to do.

"'Nothing,'" I said. "So he told me that he going to send me to America by our sister. He said by the time I got back he would have erected a small house on the back of his property, which would be mine until death.

"'America?'" I said. "'America!'" "Well, that make me laugh 'cause I had never thought of me going on an aeroplane. But I stopped laughing when he took me for passport, bought a ticket, a suitcase of dresses and pressed one thousand U.S. dollars in my hand.

"Elmina, my sister that was born just before Boyo, said that I could stay with her for a while. I hadn't seen her since she left the island decades ago, but here in America, we bonded. I was very grateful for her.

"Things first went astray when they cut the lights and she ask me to pay the bill since it three times higher since I come. Then she would buy groceries and keep them in her bedroom. She took out the TV from the living room and put that in her room, too. It didn't have place for me to stay out of her way.

"About four months after I arrived, she said that I was jeopardizing her Section 8. I asked her to explain. She said that the government pays most of the rent on the condition that she alone live there, and that the super been seeing me coming and going and he been asking questions. I didn't ask if the super seeing me coming and going from toilet to living room since I hardly ever left the apartment. She said that she putting me in a live-in babysitting work and that I would come to her place on weekends.

"The Friday of my first week she was waiting for me. She said she want to put my pay in the bank so that I would have money to take back home with me. So, every Friday, I would hand over my pay and she would give me bus tokens plus forty dollars for the week.

"The work wasn't too bad. It was only one baby. I had my own quarters that had a bedroom, kitchenette and little living room that the people furnished nice. When I closed that door in the night I used to feel like is mine. It was there that I first entertained the idea to get house. Not something in the back of Boyo, but something to my liking that I build. So I continued to give my sister the three hundred and fifty dollars a week to save. Meanwhile, I contact the St. Lucian government to see if they would deed the piece of land to me since we squat on it for so long.

"Then I met Monica. Thank God for her! She said that I should not just hand over my money to my sister because this is America where people always change. Monica said how I should ask back for my money and save it myself. I told her Elmina would be offended and I wouldn't have nowhere to go on weekends. Monica said rooms rent for fifty dollars a week.

"I ask Elmina to fetch my money from the bank. She say that she don't get home until after bank close. Then she lost her ID. Then the bank wouldn't give her the money because the signature from the new ID didn't match. She stall, and stall and stall. Finally, she got angry and call me an ungrateful wretch and said why I think that the roof over my head for two years should be free. Then she gave me a long list of dishes that she said I either break or thief and say that the money would replace her expensive things and for the weekend room and board.

"I moved into a room behind a gambling hall on Flatbush and, when police shut it down, the landlord offered me the whole place for four hundred dollars."

"Madam Lucian," I said gently. "It is four o'clock. Tell me what happened to the house."

"Every story has a beginning, Valdi. Just wait. The hall had a nice big stove and, to thank the landlord, I baked him a bread. I also gave bread to Monica and the people I was working for. Everybody say that the bread was so good, if I sold they would buy.

"Monica said charge three dollars instead of the two fifty I had been charging. When I discovered that was the price of a brick in St. Lucia I knew it was God's rainbow to me. I told Boyo what I wanted to do, and he told me to forget about the squatter plot. He bought a piece of land right next to his own and gifted that to me. He worked with an architect, drew up the plans and paid for that too. I started sending money for him to bank and he would send me regular statements. Nine years after I came to America, I told Boyo that I ready to bless the ground and start building. You may remember, Valdi, that's around the time that we met."

Yes, I remembered. I remembered Madam Lucian crying a lot 'cause she couldn't go home in person for the sod turning. She mailed a small box for Boyo with a bible from Ava, Florida Water from Monica, a candle from me and a cassava bread she wanted him to bury in the ground. Boyo mailed back a brick and a bag of dirt.

"Madam Lucian, where is the house?" I asked firmly.

"There is no house," she said defiantly.

"There is a house. I saw the pictures. You know what? I going to take you to the hospital."

"There is no house. It's not there," she was muttering now, jabbering.

"Okay. There is no house. What happened to it?"

"Boyo never built it. He lied," she said.

"But we all saw the pictures Boyo sent of the house."

"Everything since the groundbreaking was a lie. He used the land as a wager for a bet and lost it. Somebody else built on that land. It is not mine. Boyo lost his own property, too."

I didn't want to walk this betrayal road with Madam Lucian, but questions seeped between my lips and I get a mix up story that her brother's wife had called from England to say that she had left Boyo because he had gambled away everything they had, including Madam Lucian's money and land. And that he was in jail because it was illegal for St. Lucians to bet, anyhow. Madam Lucian called herself stupid for being so trusting and said that she wanted to die.

I hooked the baby under one arm, the other I put around Madam Lucian and squeezed her tightly, willing my breath into her.

"You not stupid. Is only because you illegal in this country. You couldn't travel and do it for yourself. You had to trust somebody, Madam Lucian. It's the glass prison we illegals live in, Madam Lucian, not you. Don't beat up yourself; these things happen all the time. Sometimes, it's the price we pay for trying to 'sing the Lord's song in a strange land.'"

My cell phone rang. It was Madam Lucian boss sounding frantic. He apologized for calling my cell phone, and explained that he and his wife had returned home to find no sign of Dorothé and the children. I told him that while she was with me she had begun to feel unwell, but would be there soon. I also added that she could not prepare supper for them that evening, and would be taking the next day off to go to the doctor. The phone call propelled Madam Lucian out the park.

I sat and waited in the lobby while Madam Lucian went upstairs with the children. She had gone up at 6:30 p.m., but did not come down until minutes to eight 'cause she had to feed and bathe them. I reminded her that I had already told her boss that she could not stay.

"I offered to do it. This is all I have left."

I went home by Madam Lucian and made sure she take she pressure pills, because her head was hurting real bad. I waited while she showered. To my surprise, she emerged in street clothes. She had decided to come home with me to avoid being alone.

"Call Monica, you know she will come over here and stay with you."

She said that she rather go home with me. She begged me not

to say anything about the house to the others because she did not want to depress Ava so close to her graduation, and Monica would only keep talking about it.

The next morning, I wake up to find *water-mouth* Monica in my place. She and Madam Lucian were sitting at the kitchen table looking at carpet samples for "the house." I didn't start to cuss out Monica, because Madam Lucian needed her.

Madam Lucian give me two *couya mouth* to warn me not to talk about the house. She didn't have to worry. I was afraid to open my mouth and say anything to Monica because it would turn out bad. Miz Monica *take in front.*

"Valdi, if I make confusion between you and Ava on purpose, do you think I would 'ave come 'ere in your 'ouse? Me nah want no problem."

I DON'T DO DOGS

Though the boy had been a piece of work since the business with his father, I still couldn't believe it when I came out the bathroom and found the entire contents of my handbag swimming in that big fish tank in the living room. I hold my head and bawl when my Columbia ID card, the only piece of American paper I had with my name on it, floated by. I pull up a chair to reach in to get it out but, when I remember the size of some of the fish in the tank, my nerve failed me.

I call the boy who had enough good sense left to hide. That was a good decision on his part, because I didn't trust myself with him in that moment. I called the woman who matter-of-factly said that she would send someone to drain the tank. Like that would bring back my Columbia ID, and my expired Trinidad and Tobago passport! I feel trapped. I had no ID from here that I could present and fool people, and I didn't have nothing to show I'm a damn Trinidadian either!

I stumble out the front door and collapse on the stoop. I think about my life swimming in that tank, Madam Lucian and her problems, Ava's nasty attitude, Monica's betrayal. There was not one pleasant thought to be plucked from my senseless existence. I suddenly could understand these descendants of the renaissance puffing and drinking like there was no tomorrow for them.

I stepped inside and slammed the front door loudly.

"Boy, your father is here to see you."

He swooped like a bat to the front door, his face lit up like a jolly jack-o'-lantern. The smile ebbed in slow motion as he turned and ran through the living room, down to the basement, into the kitchen calling everywhere for the father who was not there. His pain was supposed to make me feel good, but it was so pitiful that I couldn't bear to say, "I tricked you; your father not here. He's never coming back. That's what you get for messing with my stuff." Instead, I was more convinced than ever that this psycho shit could be solved with one look at the asshole.

As I stood there thinking about how to get the boy and the asshole together, he jumped on a chair and kicked me in my chest. He tried it again, but I hold him in a bear hug all the way to the bedroom. I dropped him on the bed and escaped. Once I had wedged a chair behind the bedroom door, I called the woman and told her that the boy was freaking out because he needed to see his father.

She said, "Valdi, someone will be right over to drain the tank."

"This is not about the tank, you must reunite them before somebody go to jail."

She said that she wanted nothing to do with that asshole (her word), and launched into a tirade about choosing him over the objections of her relatives. I say that the asshole (using the word, too) was the only father the boy got.

"You have two hands, two feet, a nice face and old money so you could always get another man."

"I'll ask his therapist," she said, brushing me off.

"I am going to call his father as soon as I get you off this phone."

"I forbid it. I forbid it! Don't you dare overstep!"

"Should I wait until he kill me and throw me in the fish tank, too? I am calling."

I did not pick up when she ring down the house phone and my cell phone. I call the asshole's office and got his secretary, Hannah. After a little chitchat about her people down South, I told her to tell her boss that his ex-wife humbly requests that he drop by after work because his son needs him. Hannah asked for the address and put me on hold for a few minutes.

"Valdi, there's one thing. He's gonna be there 'round about seven. He say you best be gone 'fore he gets there."

I called the part-time sitter and left for Brooklyn.

MADAM LUCIAN and her barrel of problems were sitting by the basement steps when I arrived. She followed me in and, for the first time since I knew her, I prepared something for her to eat. Lost inside our worlds, we barely spoke. At nine o'clock, I reminded her that it was getting late and she should go home, but she said that she was sleeping on the couch.

Next morning under my foot was hurting so bad that it was an hour before I tested it on the floor. I called over by the woman to see if the shit had hit the fan. She sounded light and giggly. When I mentioned my feet hurt, she said to take the day off.

I yelled "mawnin" to Madam Lucian and, when she answered, I phoned back the woman to say I would be at work.

"There are two surprises waiting when you get here. Two nice surprises," she said.

I wondered if she and the asshole had made up. I told her no surprise had ever found favor with me, but she said hers was "no big deal." She explained that my stuff was still in the tank. Since the fish had bitten into them by the time help came, it had made no sense to empty the tank.

"Don't worry, Valdi. I'll have everything replaced."

She greeted me with a tray of fresh cinnamon muffins, and led me to a rich, red leather recliner that she said was mine. She said that she could have it sent to Brooklyn if I wanted, but she would rather I left it there since she wanted me to be comfortable in her home.

"You have this uncanny way of doing the right thing. You should be a parent. I know it wasn't easy for you to call my ex, but feast your eyes on the results."

She give a loud "Ta, da!" and swung her arm wide like she was presenting a car on a game show. The boy ran into the living room with a big smile on his face. I was so relieved to see him like that. I squeezed him tight, and he apologized for feeding my papers to the fish. I sat on my red chair and reclined all the way back, the boy climbed up and sat on my lap.

"Valdi, that was the big surprise; now here is the itsy bitsy one. Close your eyes."

The woman let out a shrill whistle and a fluffy, black ball with two beady eyes and a dripping nose sailed across the floor and into the boy's lap who, it so happened, was still seated on *my* lap.

"DOG! OH GAWD! D-O-O-O-G! OH GAWD! OH GAWD! OH GAWD! DOG!"

I pushed the boy with the dog off my lap in a frenzy and stood on the seat of the recliner. Somehow, the dog's feet got caught in between my shirt buttons, as I shake, sweat and thrash the air.

The woman was screaming, "Wait!" but I didn't have time for that. My hand connected with the dog and he landed *boop* on my feet. I tried to kick him off the chair; he yelped, but would not get off the damn recliner. I stepped over to the end table and onto another chair. From there, I sped to the kitchen and jumped up onto the counter. I don't know who was screaming louder — me, the boy, the dog or the woman.

The woman came into the kitchen to ask how I could be so cruel.

"There better be no broken bones. Americans hate animal cruelty."

"But people cruelty is okay? I told you from day one, I told your husband from day one, and your son has been on enough walks with me over the past four years to know. No damn dogs! But you did not consider my feelings at all. I can't believe that you would ambush me like this."

She had started to look ashamed.

"Who knew that you would flip out over a tiny purebred? For the record, the dog was a surprise to me, too. It came here with my ex-husband yesterday. At first, I told him that the dog could not stay, because he knows that you dislike them, but when I saw my son springing to life last night, I had to let him stay. Valdi, you understand, right?"

"If the dog stays, I go."

"Valdi, we can work through this. Just give it a try."

"I cannot be here with a dog."

"We can help you adjust."

"I will not be here with a dog."

"Valdi, he's happy. I'll pay for therapist visits to help you work through this."

"Beyond that?"

"The dog works. Valdi, please be okay with this. I need you both."

After the boy and the woman had caged the dog, they left with it for the vet. I left the house and walked aimlessly through Harlem for quite a while, sure that Madam Lucian was still in my apartment. The asshole had brought that dog there for spite; it was payback for me calling him an asshole to his face. I tried to force tears so I would know that I was still here … feeling something. Nothing came.

Later, in the apartment in Brooklyn, after I had called a cab and sent Madam Lucian home, I trolled nanny postings like a hooker, promising whatever childcare virtues I figured could get me a job. Then I saw this one:

> ### Wonderful Family Seeking a Weekday Nanny
>
> *We are seeking a special person for our special family. Our oldest child had a major medical setback and is mostly confined to his stroller during the day. He needs very little and is very easy to care for.*
>
> *Our second child is in full-day school and he needs the babysitter only for daily drop-off and pick-up. Our third child will start nursery school in a couple months. She, too, would only require pick-up and drop-off and a little help with getting dressed in the morning.*
>
> *We also have a delightful baby girl who rarely cries. We are seeking the perfect nanny who will fall in love with our kids and not treat them as if they were just a paycheck. Both of us work from home, so we do require that you take the kids out during the day. We have memberships in all the major museums and a couple drop-in centers where you can expand their curious minds.*
>
> *We offer two weeks paid vacation and major holidays off. We are a fun and caring family, and we are looking for someone like us. We do not require a college education, but we do want someone with a caring heart. We want someone to be with us for years to come, not just until they decide that they don't want to do this anymore, because our kids get very attached.*
>
> *Hours are generally 7:30 a.m. to 6:00 p.m., rare evenings and occasional weekends. We do need assistance with cooking meals, light housekeeping and laundry. Our competitive salary is $350 to $400/week, depending on experience. You must have checkable references from at least one family for whom you worked for an extended period.*

It was Madam Lucian job! I called to let Madam Lucian know, but her response was so contrary that, if she weren't a Christian, I would swear she was hitting the sauce.

The woman called to say that the dog was all right — as if I cared — and apologized for springing it on me. She said she didn't know that my stuff with dogs ran so deep, and asked what had triggered my phobia. I told her that I didn't have to have a phobia to hate dogs.

"Did you ever get bitten by a dog, or did someone you love get bitten?"

"No."

"Did you have dogs when you were little?"

"My family had cats and a parrot, but we never had a dog, and the dogs running the streets never bothered me."

"Valdi, your fear is deep-seated. I called a friend who specializes in phobias. She thinks you need help. I'll take care of the cost even if you don't return to work."

I thought about advantage-takers out there posting jobs like Madam Lucian's slave work, and wanted to go back to my work where me and the woman had come to an understanding.

"I want to come back to work," I said.

"I want you to come back, too, but it's time to let someone help you."

She gave me the number to call her friend. After that, she called every day to see if I had made the appointment. I said "no."

I researched "people who hate dogs" online, and discovered my extreme reaction was called cynophobia. It made some people vomit. Even the written word "dog," could loosen bowels and make hearts race. It seems that fear of dogs could also make healthy, sensible, human beings consider or even commit suicide. The last piece of information was reassuring, because it meant that the shit between dogs and me wasn't so deep. I would kill a dog before I let it kill me.

I reached out to Ava, thinking that she could proffer a home remedy that would sail me back up the woman's stoop without a qualm, but she didn't answer. I typed in "cures for cynophobia." One doctor recommended that the affected person confront the object of the fear in the presence of a licensed psychologist. Since my problem was more like cynophobia-lite, I decided to head to Albert's Pet Shoppe and take care of this business my own damn self.

Albert's was on Nostrand Avenue; a little, dingy place near the bus stop that no one ever entered. Indeed, folks wondered if the animals were providing cover for something else. The bus stop was directly in front the store. I grabbed the door quickly before I could change my mind, and darted inside. It was dimly lit and dirty.

I walked down a narrow aisle sandwiched by rabbits, birds and rodents, and a huge macaw that flew behind me quarreling. I arrived at a long counter at the end of the aisle. At least the front of the store had light, which came from a long aquarium with ancient, grizzly fish. The spookiest part was that, up to this point, I had not seen one human. I wouldn't have been surprised to hear the door slam behind me so the thriller could begin. I had just turned around to leave when a door *did* slam. In the semi-darkness, my skin began to crawl.

"Somebody here?" I asked loudly.

"Yeah, yeah," the voice came from the left, and an old, olive man walked toward me zipping his fly.

"Sorry, I had to sheeeet," he said, grinning.

"Where the dogs at?" I asked, somewhat relieved to see him.

"Venga."

He turned back in the direction from which he had come and waved me forward. I couldn't move my foot once I realized that a dog was less than six feet away.

"Don't let it out," I said apprehensively.

"Cálmate, chica. Él es solamente un pequeño perrito," the man said, trying to reassure me.

Small dog or not, my heart began to race.

The man went back to the counter, picked up a flashlight and shone it into the cage, which was directly opposite to where I stood. Inside, I could make out the outline of a little, *maga* dog.

"No water," I say to the man, pointing to the overturned bowl.

He cursed the dog for overturning the bowl, and walked over to the cage. By the time he had clicked the latch open, I had vanished behind the counter and snapped the security gate shut. He filled the water bowl from the bathroom and offered it to the grateful dog. When he noticed me behind the counter, he said I should come out, *pronto!* I closed my eyes and walked toward where I figured the dog cage was and then forced them open. It stared at me. It stood on its hind legs and asked to come out. The dog was black and had only one ear and I felt something like sadness — something that made me feel to cuddle it. It whimpered.

"He like you. You want? No much money. One ears," the man said.

"I do not want it." I said.

I don't know what part of that sentence the man didn't understand, but he bent down and clicked the cage. I made the mental leap, but my feet wouldn't go even when he was pushing the dog in my face.

"You buy? Hold heem."

CONFRONT THE OBJECT OF YOUR FEAR!!!!

"NO!!!" I screamed, but the man couldn't hear me, 'cause the sound was only in my head.

"He no bite."

Water gushed from every hole in my body, the biggest gush seeping down my legs. The man didn't know 'cause I was wearing pants. He pushed the dog into my arms that refused to drop it, and it burned my face with its tongue. Its fur prickled like thorns. I screamed this time, sending out a piercing sound. Its echo, circling the room, made the man jump and the dog flee. He scampered under the aquarium on three legs.

"¡Eres loca!" the man screamed. "You keeeel mi perro." He jack me up against the counter.

"I pay," I said, opening my handbag and handing him an envelope with many weeks' pay.

"I catch heem for you."

I was probably on the sidewalk before he even got to his knees to look for the dog. I kept running past maybe ten bus stops before I collapsed and rolled into a drain somewhere in front the butcher shop.

AN OXYGEN MASK was on my face, and I was lying on a gurney in the hospital.

"Do you know who you are?" I heard someone say. I did not respond.

Do you know who you are?

When no one was watching, I get up from the bed and walk out the front entrance. I went home, washed the butcher water off me and sat on the frog-skin leather couch. The woman called. She said she had made the appointment for me at two o'clock the next day. I told her that I wanted to go now, so she put me on hold to call the friend.

It turned out that I knew the psychologist, because I used to take the twins on play dates at her house.

"How is your daughter?" I mumbled. She said that the girl was going to school in Paris. I asked how she was coping with that.

"It's an opportunity for both of us to learn and grow. Life calls for us to handle challenges with maturity. It's just the way it is." She was talking about me.

"What if it is too hard?"

She got up from her chair and moved to the couch, curling one leg under her. She patted the seat next to her. At least she didn't think my stuff warranted lying down. She asked when in my childhood I had become aware that I disliked dogs. I told her that I was never exposed to dogs back home. She said that she found that strange, because she had visited many Caribbean villages and dogs seem to roam the streets freely. I couldn't come up with one neighbor with a dog, or a stray that roamed the area, or a relative with a dog. I told her that dogs weren't a part of my life in Trinidad and that is why I had such an aversion to them in America.

"I see," she said. But I knew that she didn't see at all.

"You were never bitten as a child?"

"Only by mosquitoes."

"Valdi, is there an incident you can think of that may have led to these feelings you have toward dogs? Feelings that are putting your job, maybe even your life, in jeopardy."

I told her that nothing dramatic had ever happened before the pet shop, and gave a watered down version of the day's events.

"Your fear deepens every time you encounter a dog, so it will take some time to get you well. We'll have weekly sessions during which we'll address your fear rationally. You must be very strong to survive as a babysitter in Dogtown, USA."

I figured that the treatment would take a long time, so I asked when I would be able to return to work. She said that she would give me medication so I could go back right away.

She picked up a prescription pad and started writing. I asked for the "no name" brand as I had no health insurance. She picked up a bunch of keys and opened the top drawer of her filing cabinet. She took out a big handful of pills and placed them on her desk; she gave me all the ones in the purple packs.

"The day you go back to work, take two of these four hours before you walk through the door. Then take one every four hours for two weeks. This will help you to control your emotions toward the dog. Maybe you may even grow to like him."

I felt ill.

"I can't do it."

"Valdi, changing your reality begins here," she said tapping her head. "When you're in the dog's presence and your heart begins to race, look at him and see him as a cat. For you, visualization is critical. Get some old films with dogs, like *Lassie,* where people interact with dogs in normal, calm, everyday circumstances."

I knew that no amount of visualization could make me watch a pitchfork and see a spade. Hopelessness hugged me like a coarse blanket.

She got up, signaling that the visit was over.

"Your visit is completely confidential. My license is staked on confidentiality. I'll see you in a week. Remember, fear is a learned behavior. It's time for you to teach yourself otherwise."

BREATHING INSIDE THE GATE

"I'm blessed, and highly favored," Madam Lucian beamed though the phone. I regretted taking the call because she quickly forget her state of blessed, high favor to accuse me of hiding inside when she came to my place. I was probably out when she dropped by, but nothing I said to Madam Lucian could convince her that she didn't hear me shuffling around inside.

"If you were not home, tell me where you went!"

"Madam Lucian, if I was home, I would have opened the door. But, suppose I was home and didn't want company; what is so wrong about that?"

"Ah ha, I ketch you! Sounds like selfishness to me. I will not be coming back by you."

"Madam Lucian that's your choice. I know I have been a friend to you, even holding your secret when I don't see what wrong with telling people the damn house gone. And who is thinking about my problems? Thanks to your friend Monica, my friendship with Ava is over."

"Ava got graduation tickets for Monica and me," Madam Lucian said. "We will be front and center, tomorrow."

The glee in her voice was unmistakable. All this time I know Madam Lucian, she been *fronting* sunshine. I never thought she could be so wicked. She had to know that piece of information would cut deep. It was almost like she wanted to punish me for knowing the truth about her blasted house, when pure happenstance had placed me at Sherman the day she lost everything.

I tell Madam Lucian that my friendship with Ava is seventeen years old and would eventually survive this so, ticket or not, I was going to the graduation. I barely said goodbye before I hung up the phone on Madam Lucian. I imagined her sitting in the dark, muttering my name over a big black cauldron, giggling with she no-teeth self. She had taken to walking the road without her *mouth plates.* The way she was *haunted* these days, I wouldn't put it past her to come back to my house. Since I didn't want to be there deliberating whether or not to open the door, I walked up Utica Avenue to get my nails done and put on a fresh weave for Ava's graduation. It was only when I stop by the liquor store and buy a big bottle of fine brandy, I realize that I intended to go to Ava's party, too.

I didn't know whether I was more disturbed by the easy camaraderie among the stylists at the salon or by the emptiness I felt at the gulf of estrangement that was widening between Ava and me. By nightfall, I was in pieces.

It didn't matter if I rocked the hairstyle, or if the Asian lady painted Joseph's dream coat on my nails or if I walked along Fifth Avenue swinging ten shopping bags. Not one of those things was a Social Security Number or a pathway to a normal life in this America. It was like gathering rats and a huge pumpkin for the ball, all the while knowing that there was no fairy Godmother to turn the rats into coachmen and the pumpkin into a carriage.

My daily routine was reduced to tiny, inconsequential motions on the curb of other people's lives, and I dare not approach the gate. I could paint the gate, scrub the sidewalk, sweep the garbage, but I dare not pass through the gate. Sitting by that statue, I could pontificate until "thy kingdom come" about the black man who going to be president, but could I vote for him? Could he accept the illegal dollars I earn minding young Americans—like I am their damn mother—as a campaign contribution? And if I still had them, could I show my tattered Columbia ID card or my expired passport as I enter a government building without feeling that they about to lock me up and deport me? Shit, I want to breathe *inside* the gate.

Like Ava.

Sitting there in the illegal basement, on the frog-skin leather couch, I crack open Ava's bottle of brandy and tek a swig. I remember she ask me once about my plans for my future. First, I laugh in she face, and then I tell her that the only thing I could plan without papers is an exit strategy out of the people country. She had said that my attitude was defeatist because, if I trained all my energies towards a Green Card, I would attract one. Like Monica, Ava say.

First, I tell her if she had really been my friend, she would have asked Uncle Ram to marry me and fix my papers long before Monica came on the scene. I also said that if that New Age "attract-what-you-want-and-it-will-come" bullshit was true, America would be stuffed with the world's billions who dreamed of being successful in America, while their home countries lay empty. Ava said millions without legal status still managed to make their dreams come through.

"If Madam Lucian chooses to live out her days in America, she could build an empire, just by baking bread. Valdi, just look at that mansion that that old woman has constructed in St. Lucia," Ava said. "You, however, refuse to tap into your talents and embark on some fruitful commercial enterprise. Write a book, do something ... anything! My best advice to you is to spruce up, lose twenty pounds, powder your face, wear perfume instead of them greasy culture oils, and wear heels instead of flats. Do it consistently, Valdi, not only when you want to shake yourself out of a slump. Maybe you will meet a man on the bus who will marry you and make you straight."

At the time, I had told her she talking shit, but she said that she could say what the hell she want, and nobody could put her out of America. With that, she gave me a smug "put that in your pipe and smoke it" look.

I swig she brandy again.

To Ava, who came to America and won. I, Valdi, drink to that. To Ava, who leaving babysitting with legal resident status. I, Valdi, drink to that. To Ava, who will now wear her high heels to a bona fide government job. I, Valdi, swig to that. To Ava, who will obtain her laude-da degree tomorrow. I, Valdi, take a big swig on that one. To Ava ....

I KNEW IT WAS Ava's graduation day when I awoke, because the sun was bright and high in the sky; perfect weather for perfect Ava. And I was stale drunk. I took the longest shower of my life, applied make-up, especially under-eye concealer, and wide-eye-opener to minimize the brandy damage. I liberally sprayed a couple of them perfumes Ava had given me over the years. Then I packed my behind into a size eight eggshell pantsuit to mek my little, red, lace camisole pop. I emptied everything from my everyday pocketbook onto the center table and transferred a few basic items to my red

Coach purse. I tumbled my red, high-heeled sandals from the box and, in short order, had stepped from the basement into the light.

Halfway up Utica, I turn 'round and hustle back down the hill and climb down into the basement, 'cause to face Ava success was to face my fucking failure. The pills that the doctor give me was in the pile of stuff I had emptied from my purse. I swallowed three. They were intended to help me cope with dogs and, today I would be meeting three: Madam Lucian, Monica and, that friggin'pit bull, Ava. I drank two cups of coffee with a little tip of brandy before I attempted the ascent again. The second attempt was the trick.

I found pleasure in the gentle sun and calm breeze and the knowledge that it was my best friend Ava's big day. We were going to celebrate. Everything was moving in slow motion around me. I floated into the dollar store to buy a pair of slippers. I drifted along Eastern Parkway, swinging my red sandals, perching on this bench and that. I chuckled loudly as I recall what the old people say home, "Happy like Pappy." *Not my Pappy.* Oops! A thought about father had drifted into my sanctuary, but I firmly turned my mind to dear, sweet Ava.

Suppose Ava is upset to see me?

W-h-a-t-e-v-e-r.

Suppose when I see Monica I box she in the mouth for talking about that essay?

W-h-a-t-e-v-e-r.

Suppose the woman choose the dog over me?

W-h-a-t-e-v-e-r.

Thoughts about how Ava didn't give me a graduation ticket and hadn't asked if I was coming to her party were making my head throb.

W-h-a-t-e-v-e-r, my new best friend, took care of that thought, too.

Abruptly, I zeroed in on my surroundings. I was at Bedford and Eastern Parkway, three blocks from the college. I leaned on a lamp-post and put back on my high heels, dropped the slippers in the garbage and clicked-clicked down the hill to Medgar Evers College.

I was still a block-and-half away when I noticed that people were hanging from their windows as hundreds lined the streets below. I see something like a swarm of *corbeaux* pecking frantically at a carcass, frenziedly jostling each other for a bite. Then I realize that it was the hats of the graduates bobbing in the breeze. It was just like black folks to make a spectacle of everything. The pomp and circumstance of commencement exercises at revered institutions like my alma mater, Columbia University, was certainly not this rowdy.

Is Columbia U. still your alma mater if you were kicked out?
W-h-a-t-e-v-e-r.

Medgar Evers College graduates were prancing in the streets like it was some *jouvay* band for carnival. I scramble onto a sanitation bin where I could see them *jamming* their way up Bedford Avenue. The faculty was leading, most of them showing off their robes with the deep, deep hoods I once thought would be mine.

W-h-a-t-e-v-e-r.

Ava was next in line. She held a huge American flag as she walked in the midst of a pounding African drum-line.

I clap, I clap, I clap. I scream. Pure joy in my heart because my friend reach, and she hit them hard. Another immigrant who had to stoop to conquer and still manage to mop the floor with Americans. I climb off the bin and run down the street, catching the procession just as it suddenly veered to the left towards the school's side gate. There, I buck up 'pon a barricade.

"Avaaaaah," I screamed. She didn't hear me, though people next to her look around.

"Avaaaaaaaaaah!"

The procession gathered speed, the faculty disappearing into the side gate. Someone touched Ava's shoulder and pointed to me. She see me but, before she could respond, the crush propelled her into the gate. I follow the top of the flag for as long as I could. I watch the rest of the parade and then walk to the front of the college to figure out a way to get inside. Someone touched me. Monica.

Madam Lucian, still with she no-teeth self, inserted her body between us like a referee. She was good *boldface* because, in that moment, her *standing* with me was not much better than Monica's. I couldn't even look at Madam Lucian. She just look dirty. Even her hair looked like she soak it in dirty water before she come.

"Madam Lucian, you okay?"

"Well, I not dead."

"Valdi, long time me eyes nuh light 'pon yuh. You look nice," Monica said awkwardly.

I swept her from head to toe and from toe to head taking in the knee high boots, wool dress and hat, elbow gloves — all in perfect pink. Perfect make-up, perfect hair, perfect nails, perfect gossipmonger. Uncle Ram might think he have Monica in grip, but I could see the life was oozing from he 401k.

Monica say sorry for what she had done without elaborating, and offer me her ticket to the ceremony. But that was just too easy for she, 'cause we both know that she just had to stand there looking cute and the college president 'self would invite her in. Maybe even give her a seat next to him on the podium. I tore the ticket until there was nothing more to hold.

"But, Valdi, why you do that? Monica making peace."

Monica looked relieved like she had expected my reaction to be much worse.

"Valdi, see that you ah tear up my ticket, we just ah 'ave to stay outside together. Is best we ah go near the side gate where the procession went it. Then we ah peep through the fencing at the ceremony. Ava said everything ah 'appen outside. Madam Lucian, you 'ave ticket, so go through the front door and get a seat. We will meet you in dis same spot when everything done."

Madam Lucian said that she not going inside if the two of us staying outside, and she tear up her ticket too. As we walked, Monica teased Madam Lucian for being so dramatic. She had her arm around Madam Lucian and both of them look at me and give me a wink eye. If water wasn't already riding high over the bridge, that moment would have felt like old times.

We selected a spot behind the wooden fence that bordered the amphitheater. As I was about to sit down, Monica pointed out that my pants white. She volunteered to go to the store across the street and buy some chairs. I gave her my wallet and tell her to use what she needed. Then I sat on the ground anyway. Monica returned with three chairs and a plastic tablecloth that she spread on the ground. Then she put down a six-pack of beer wrap up in newspaper, a tub of fry chicken, a can of ginger ale, and some snacks. She gave me back my wallet, and I didn't have to open it to know she had not spent a penny of my money. Uncle Ram credit card balance must have jumped a bit.

Monica said that when she came out of the store she saw Ava's family step out of a limo in front the college. "Me see dem; was Ava two bosses, dem parents on both sides, plus de six children."

Anger in tiny wisps rose in me at the idea that the outsiders would be seated daintily inside, and we, the insiders, would be sitting outside the gate. Monica handed Madam Lucian a ginger ale and gave me a beer. Madam Lucian said she wanted a beer, too.

"Blood fire! You ever drink beer, Christian lady? Ah wha you ah ask for dat for?" Monica said.

"Is just for today; is Ava's graduation," Madam Lucian replied.

"Ah nah give you no beer. Madam Lucian you ah too old for alco-ol. I open wan soda for you already. Drink dat and satisfy. Nuh so, Valdi?"

"How I get involved with dat?"

"Should Madam Lucian drink alco-ol?"

"Open the damn beer and give her, she deserves at least that."

Madam Lucian shot me a warning glance. I deflect it with a *sweet-eye.* She burst out into one of her joyous peals of laughter. Monica laughed, too. And, if I had laughed, it *would* have been like old times.

The drone of their voices behind me and the warmth of the plastic tablecloth beneath me put me to sleep. So when the time came for the president to announce the valedictorian, Monica had to wake me so I could listen to what Ava have to say. But, first, the president boast and boast about his valedictorian. He described a stellar, part-time student who paid her way through college with a babysitting job.

That wasn't strictly true.

He said that this student's leadership and advice was revered, not only by young students, but by himself, the administration, faculty, and board of governors. Indeed, anyone who was privileged enough to know her welcomed her advice.

Except me.

He said that the student had poured her entire essence into her academic pursuits and had "indelibly sewn herself into the social and cultural fabric of the institution." He went on to say that it was for these reasons that she was graduating today with a 4.0 GPA and the top academic prizes in five departments."

I joined Monica and Madam Lucian by their hole in the fence. He hadn't even named the student, but the faculty and the graduates were already on their feet. The president had to beg them to sit down.

"The faster order is restored, the quicker you will hear from this student who represents the best of what Medgar Evers College attempts to infuse into its students. This student will change many minds as she grows. Now, I invite the participants of Medgar Evers

College's thirty-first Grand Convocation to join me as I welcome our valedictorian, Miss Vasumati Baldeosingh."

"Vasumati!?" All three of us say that simultaneously, looking at each other in surprise.

"Madam Lucian, Ava nah say she is valedictorian?"

"That's the word she used," Madam Lucian said.

"And they nah call someone name Vasumati?"

"That's the name they call."

"But dat ah make no sense, unless Ava name Vasumati. Aye, Valdi, does Ava name Vasumati?"

Truth came blossoming from the bud of betrayal. Fuck! I was not floating now, 'cause the truth hit me as clear as if I had signed that bitch birth paper myself. Ava was simply "Vasumati" with an "A" put in front the first syllable of her name, with the Indian "sumati" dropped to mek it sound more American. In almost two decades of knowing Ava, she had never once told me her real name was Vasumati.

I waited for "whatever" to wash the slate clean, but it would not come and disinfect what felt like a fundamental betrayal of our friendship. After all, was not a person's name the doorway to her or his spirit? Nausea washed over me as I realized that Vasumati had never valued our friendship enough to open her doorway to me and let our spirits dance.

Monica and Madam Lucian were chattering excitedly. "Valdi, Ava's name *is* Vasumati. Look, ah she ah walk on 'pon the stage."

Monica looked at me, and her excitement vanished as she saw my ashen face. She was feeling me. Madam Lucian, too.

"Maybe Ava was a home name. Sometimes home names get so real people have to struggle to remember their real names. Look, just the other day someone asked me my name. Did I say Dorothé? No. I say Madam Lucian. Then I correct myself. A name mean nothing; it's not the person, it's only a handle for the person. Ava just forget to tell you … us."

Then both of them jostle each other at the fence to catch a glimpse of Vasumati. Vasumati who had left me at the doorway to her soul like an intruder.

All skin teeth is not grin.

Hands trembling, I hastily dropped three more pills on my tongue, and swilled them down with beer.

Vasumati's voice filled the amphitheater and spilled over the fence. I couldn't process what she said or didn't say, because I was really no longer there. But, later, in the post mortem to the after-party, after all hell had broken loose and the chain of events sent her whimpering to her bedroom, I would hear from Monica and Madam Lucian that Vasumati had asked her white family to stand for applause. The oldest child, decked out in his full military captain's uniform, presented her with a bouquet that was almost as tall as Ava. At least, so Monica say.

But, in the moment itself, slumped on the grass, I couldn't see, hear or feel anything about what Ava-sumati was saying. After the graduation ceremony, Madam Lucian roused me and said that we should try to find Ava.

"We must tell her that we feel proud ah she, 'cause she raise all we noses from off the ground."

Now, I didn't mind nothing. We didn't find Ava but, as we walked back to the bus stop, a limo breezed by. Monica said it was the one that Ava's family had come in and she was sure she had a glimpse of Ava inside.

"At least she coulda called one of our cell phones," Monica sniffed.

Whatever!

Of the four of us, Vasumati had the best place. Her apartment was legal according to New York City Building Codes, meaning she had proper exits. With my short, narrow doorway, I would broil if a fire ever touched my place on Midwood. Vasumati had central heating, and Madam Lucian had an old portable crank-up that she dragged from room to room. Vasumati had a spacious, seven-room apartment, whereas Monica's single room had been partitioned into three with curtains. We all had vermin, especially Madam Lucian, because of the restaurant downstairs and the rubbish on Flatbush Avenue. Butterflies, birds, chipmunks and squirrels played on Vasumati's windowsill.

Vasumati's apartment was on the ground floor of a three-story, walk-up in Bedstuy. A winding, cobblestone pathway, enclosed by a hedgerow, flowers and stoneware pots led to an emerald entryway with water running through copper chains that framed both sides of the front door.

Every year, Vasumati installed Santas for Christmas and jack-o'-lanterns for Halloween. She put up green curtains for St. Patrick's Day, and Old Glory on the fourth of July, Presidents' and Memorial Day. She had a yellow ribbon wound tight around a tree in honor of the troops in Iraq. Every August when the West Indian carnival energy swirl 'round in the air, and the sounds of a *pan side* practicing blocks away seeped under she door, I asked she, "Ava, what? No costume for *jouvay*?"

Sometimes she ignored me, other times she gave a curt answer, "Valdi, this is America. I belong to an American Evangelical congregation, this ethnic stuff is not for me."

When I teased her about throwing money behind improving property that wasn't hers, she puffed up and said that I set my sights too low.

"It's about pride. My surroundings reflect my standards, and I intend to own this building one day. The area has already begun to emerge. Everywhere in Brooklyn is changing for the better," Ava said excitedly.

"Emerge from what?"

One day she had launched into a long story about two men she overheard discussing the neighborhood.

"They said, 'Brooklyn is too close to Manhattan to have so many niggers,'" Ava repeated.

I asked her if she didn't have a problem with that. She said that the men were not ridiculing people with brown skin, per se, just their mentality. When I said that I still didn't get why she agreed with the statement, she assumed the tone she reserved for those she considered very stupid people.

"Valdi, I am all for developers constructing nice buildings and attracting decent people from Manhattan. Look how that Jamaican skunk, Milton, used to urinate in my hydrangeas every time he came home drunk. Since he was evicted and those nice college students moved upstairs, I no longer have that problem."

"Dem students probably burning meth over your head," I said.

"As long as they are not urinating in my hydrangeas," she retorted smugly.

A FEW HOURS AFTER the graduation, I parted the shrubs in front Ava's window and yelled, "Avaaaaaah, yuh dey?"

I knew that what she called my *"commonness"* would irritate her. I counted backwards from four, expecting the door to fly open, as was customary. Ava didn't disappoint. She appeared midway into the count, but there were no dimples threatening the rigidity of her jaw.

"Valdi, I have expressed to you on numerous occasions that I do not encourage such commonness at my abode."

I laughed with my teeth. She looked right and left and then yanked me inside, holding the front of my red, lace camisole.

"Valdi, I not going to tell you again about your behavior. And what are you doing here anyway?"

"You look nice," I offered, sweeping her from her Shirley Temple hairdo to her white, high-heeled, fur-lined mules. She was still wrapped in a silky white robe, but I could tell the end result would be dazzling. I adjusted an errant ringlet hanging down the center of her forehead. She slapped my hand away and clipped-clipped towards her bedroom.

"Who did your make-up?"

"You still haven't detailed the reason for this uninvited and unwelcomed appearance."

"I came to help you set up for the party."

"My family dispatched a company to take care of the details," she said, sweeping her arm from dainty origami butterflies to silver chafing dishes.

"You must need something," I said, planting my tired self on her Egyptian-styled armchair.

"Valdi, get off my chair with your muddy self!" I looked down and realized that the whole left side of my pants was dirty.

"Where you been anyway? Why you didn't bathe before coming here? Aren't those the same clothes you were wearing this morning?"

"I thought you didn't see me."

"You *did* run down the street screaming my name."

I let Vasumati know that I had to look like this because I sat in the dirt during the ceremony since she didn't give me, Valdi of all people, a ticket.

I had moved directly behind her as she sat before her Pulaski Edwardian mirror. She dipped a brush in blush, tapped it on a sheet of Kleenex on the counter, and passed it nervously over her perfect cheeks.

"Valdi, just detail the circumstances that bring you here. But use bullet points."

"I come to discuss what Monica said, so there would be no discomfort at the party. But since I here alone with you, how come you never tell me that your real name is Vasumati?"

"That is what you want to talk about?"

She seem taken aback, like she thought I had finally come to pay homage for her achievements.

"Valdi, get out! Go home!"

"Ava, let's thrash this out so we could be cool at the party."

"If you come to the party, we don't need to speak. I will have a lot of friends here. I don't plan to associate exclusively with any one sector," she said.

I leaned forward and jammed my chin into her left-side clavicle. She winced, but remained focused on her face in the mirror.

"Ava, haven't I been a good friend to you?"

She jumped off the stool knocking me straight onto the floor, then leaned over and pointed her finger in my face.

"You told people that you wrote papers for me."

"Just Monica."

"Same thing."

"Look, the conversation lasted a couple seconds. Monica embellished it."

"You opened the door, because jealously eating you."

"I've been holding a degree for over twenty years. You now get yours. I am two semesters away from my M.A." I scrambled to my feet and spat my words at Ava.

"Your degree is worthless, because all you do is sit on your fat ass everyday by Sherman's statue not nursing one goal."

My legs trembled. I make to sit on Ava's leather stool, but she kick it away. I fell flat on my back. She straddle me and say that I lazy. She said that I liked being illegal because it cover up my laziness. She said that Madam Lucian wanted a house; she built one. Monica wanted to be straight; she married a man who could sponsor her. That wretch went on to say that I spent twenty years complaining, "as if babysitting isn't honest bread." She said that I like a wet bag of sand around everybody neck. That final crack pierce me through and through.

"Get out of my house! And if you are planning to come to my party, take a bath!"

That's when she get up from straddling me, and say that now she had to bathe all over again. I was this close to breaking something in Vasumati's place, but something say, "Doh do that. She will take that as a reason to give people why she don't want anything to do with you."

The friendship was over, but I wasn't going out so. Later, I would take the microphone and, instead of toasting Vasumati, I would tell everybody about her exploits with her man employer. Is better Ava did beat me with a stick. I face this way and that and, though I been in that apartment many times over, I couldn't remember where to find the door.

Suddenly, Ava's tone softened, "Valdi, it's not too late for you to find yourself. Hold dreams, but set goals. Foster ideas, but court discipline."

"None of that is a Green Card," I said.

"And a Green Card is nothing without responsibility, stick-to-it-ness, passion, optimism, desire, hope, confidence and courage. None of which you have demonstrated since we met."

As she flung open the door, her voice was low, because she did not want the neighbors to hear. But, by the roaring in my head, she might as well have been screaming.

"Valdi, don't drift into my hydrangeas; stay on the cobblestones. Oh, and add good attitude to the list, a Green Card is nothing without that. Remember, if you plan to come here tonight, come with a good attitude."

I ENCOUNTERED MONICA FIRST. Her greeting was effusive, but she did not stick around because the effect of the cat suit only worked when she walked. Madam Lucian buried her head in my chest when she said hello, as if that could cover the scent of rum. Ava eyes swept over me disdainfully like manure on the ground. It didn't matter because, by midnight, she would see who really feeling like shit.

I hang a bit with some long time sitters from E. 72nd days, but all they talked about was how de children bad, white women crazy and the workload unreasonable. No amount of illustration and shenanigans could make that old babysitter story sound fresh.

Ava didn't even look at the babysitters as she nested with folks coated in professorial airs. Even Madam Lucian had something different going on because she was fielding questions about the house from her old bread customers. I stayed in the shadows listening as Madam Lucian took each questioner on a stroll through different areas of the expansive property located on "Parcel No. 84, Map Sheet 1624 B, in the registration quarter of Micoud." She threw back her head, sending her old, melodious laughter rippling through the room. Her face glowed with accolades of a job well done, and it come to me that Madam Lucian had built a new house with bricks from her imagination. I couldn't watch anymore. I focused on the college students from upstairs who had taken over the dance floor. I went back to the E. 72nd Group, but they were still talking white folks bad.

I sneaked up to the DJ booth behind Lance who was dusting off an LP. He prided himself on being the only set in Brooklyn still spinning strictly records and toting turntables. I tiptoed behind him, pressed up against him and tightened my arms around his belly. He played "who is it" for a minute and then swung me around with a broad smile that froze, cracked and vanished. Lance allowed two icicles to fall from his lips, "Whappenin', Valdi?"

He turned back to his records before I had even answered. Ava said that he had described me as quicksand sucking a brother into the ground. He made a big show of whistling at Monica across the room. She pushed out she bottom for him. Monica's antics had Uncle Ram looking sour.

Some Green-Card marriage. I had warned Monica about that. I clinked the ice in my glass as I tried to figure out what next to do. For all her big show that she had no time for me, I noticed that Ava was shadowing me anxiously. I gulped down the drink in my hand and went back to the bar.

"Give me something different again," I tell the barman.

He put two healthy shots, and filled it with something blue. I opened the front door and walked outside because that was something new to do. Through the gold blinds I could make out fuzzy shapes of people in the room. I tried to decipher who the people were. I got so caught up in my new game that I didn't see when Ava's bosses walked up the winding path. It was the shadow of the man that I recognized, a tall strapping image, with petite ones clinging onto each arm. I put the blue drink to my mouth, drained it and headed inside.

"Give me something new again."

Everyone in the party was focused on Ava and her two bosses. Lance opened the official part of the evening with a sixties record, Leslie Gore's *It's my party*. Instantly, the chorus popped into my mind: I'*ll cry if I want to ... you would cry too if it happened to you."* On cue, Ava burst into tears.

Lance gave a microphone to the man. He said that Ava had made him and his wife very happy. "She had to for me to cross the Brooklyn Bridge at all, let alone twice in one day."

Two ushers wheeled in a huge, blown-up copy of her degree and placed it behind the three of them. Pictures were taken. Ava thanked her bosses for everything and, most of all, for sharing their children. She said that if she never had children in life, thanks to them, she was certain that she had known what it was to feel a mother's love. She said she had news to share and this was the time, as bitter and sweet was occupying the same place, and beginnings were not possible without endings. She said a lot more, but it came out rambling, as she stumbled over her fancy words looking confused and conflicted.

She kept glancing at me. At first I thought she was warning me to behave, but it was in the old familiar way as if she wanted my support.

"Ava, what's the news?" somebody bawl out, anxious to get the party started again.

Ava's boss began shaking like she had *malcady*. Her husband dropped Ava's hand and clutch his wife's waist, digging his fingers into her side like he was sending his own warning.

"Ava, may we please speak privately?" he asked.

Black folks, *smelling agouti in the woods,* called out for the big news. The woman touched Ava and whispered. It almost seemed as though Ava shrugged her hand away. Ava took the microphone and thanked everyone for coming. Then she announced her job at the Board of Education as a school psychologist, and her new boss stepped forward as the babysitters in the room erupted in cheers and tears.

The woman grabbed Ava. "We must talk about this!"

"I'm sorry; later, after the party," Ava said.

The woman was talking softly, but I know she was pushing. I could hear Ava pleading to leave the plantation. She said she would stay on until the twins' first day of school. She said that she had a great, part-time nanny waiting to start.

"We have news, too. We're having another baby."

"But I have my degree now."

"I will not let you go. We forbid it," the woman insisted.

The man tried to tell the wife that this was not the time for discussion, as though you could send a hurricane packing. The woman tell Ava new boss that his job offer was no longer pertinent, and promised to match the salary Ava was being offered.

Ava said that she already made more as a babysitter. Feelings of loss and grayness came over me like the day that Madam Lucian's dream died. Like the day I ran through the park with the pink paper in my hand. I walked over and touched Ava. First, she watched me like she don't know me, and then she grabbed on to me, her tongue darting in and out of her mouth in search of words.

"You done ah pay her more. It not about the money," Monica say.

The woman's words clinked like ice blocks into an enamel basin. "Ava, I paid for your studies for the benefit of *my* family. You cannot leave us now."

Babysitters edge closer and form a ring around Ava. Her employers, old and new, in fact, all Ava white friends ease out the door.

The party finish right there! Ava barricaded herself in her room and fêters stripped the place bare of everything but the caviar. They left with armloads of food, drinks and even origami butterflies. Monica, Madam Lucian and I hung around in case Ava came out. Madam Lucian had bad feelings and vomited. Monica said that her pressure was probably high and escorted her home to get her medication.

I put a Sam Cooke CD on Ava stereo, and sat in the darkness listening. Two hours later, no sign of Ava. I bit a bright red apple and, though its sweet nectar filled my mouth, I dropped it back on the table and left.

BETTER SERVED IN LIQID

The morning after Ava's party, I called Chloë and told her that I ready to come back to work. She said as long as I was taking therapy, she was certainly willing to try. She said the past week had reminded her how much I kept her afloat and that Harlem has been lonely without me. I said I wanted to start immediately. She told me the boy was with his father, and would be back home about midday.

She paused for a long time. "Valdi, are you really okay with this?"

I delivered a curt "yes," unable to say more.

I could hear the doubt in her voice, so I injected a lethal dose of good spirits this time.

"I am s-o-o-o totally fine with the dog. My treatment is working."

I was going to add that I was well enough to walk Tennis in an emergency, but my tongue refused to bend for that lie.

"Valdi, what about when you two go out? Cole won't leave Tennis behind."

A hot liquid bubbled in my head. I suggested that she hire a dog walker to walk both the dog and the boy.

"Valdi, you're joking, right? Do you need another week?"

I closed my eyes and evoked Lassie in *Lassie's Gift of Love,* before I could answer.

"I told you that I got this," I said, the calmness in my voice belying my terror.

I would head uptown immediately, because I read on the Internet that it was better to arrive before the hostile dog in order to establish territory. Plus, I had some ideas of my own to keep him at bay. I put the extra boxed set of *Lassie* I had purchased in Harlem in my bag and swallowed the required two pills, plus one-and-a-half. The dose would last at least for the train ride.

THE SMELL OF DOG wrapped me tight, as I kept my eye out for him. I know he wasn't there ... but still. In the bathroom, I peed into a Styrofoam cup. I went back to the front door and, backing back in a straight line, I drip couple drops of pee on the floor all the way to my red leather recliner. Woolly strands of disgusting tufts of its hair were plastered on the chair's seat and arms. It was clear that the animal had established his territory down to the very last detail.

I wiped down my chair and everything in that house with disinfectant. I vacuumed from attic to basement. I stripped beds; washed linen; scrubbed the bathroom and took a long shower. I take the Styrofoam cup back to the chair and created a rectangle of pee to fence off my chair. I take two more pills, inserted a *Lassie* DVD and waited.

Between sleep and wake, I see Lassie bring worms for an owl with a broken wing that was minding its egg. Then I see Lassie taking a child's doll to the police station to warn police that the doll's owner is in a ditch that is filling up with water.

Keys in the front door! I pause the DVD, pull up my legs and stick my hands under my bottom. The little boy calls my name. I try to push "yes" out my throat. The door slammed BLAM! The boy run in and pelt himself on me. I ain't see or hear the dog yet, but I know it there!

I unpaused the DVD to focus on the only dog I could deal with — one that is immortalized on film, doing good works. Lassie has arrived at the police station and is gently pawing an officer's coat. They get into the front seat of the squad car to go and rescue the little girl who, by now, has water up to her shoulders.

The real dog barks furiously at the front door.

The squad car arrives; Lassie is barking directions at the officers, as they run to the ditch.

The real dog enters the room. The boy opens his mouth.

"If you call that dog over here, I will go home!"

The real dog pauses and stiffens.

I drag my eyes to the television but couldn't follow what Lassie was doing because my heart speed up buh-bop, buh-bop, buh-bop. Water coat my skin, and the trembling start. At least the sensations were muted now, like getting stick with a pinhead instead of needles. I feel like I projecting the appearance of deadly calm.

The real dog start edging closer, spraying as he walks. He arrives at the rectangle surrounding my chair. I ask the boy if I am smiling, and he nods. The dog didn't come in the rectangle and I didn't go out of it. For the rest of the afternoon, the boy did my bidding.

"Pass me my handbag and a glass of water."

"Answer that phone, it's probably your mother."

The boy snuggled with me on the red chair to watch the other Lassie episodes. He wanted to know what had happened to the color on the TV. So I told him about my small days when TV was black and white and, in Trinidad, we had only Channels 2 and 13, both showing the same program. I told him how, on Sunday evenings, after my sister and I had had a bath by the water barrel, we would watch *Lassie* at six o'clock.

The dog wept that I had both his chair and his boy. It just fixed me with its beady eyes. Finally, Chloë came home.

I KNEW BETTER THAN to ever turn my back on that dog. I took to walking backwards when it was behind me, which was often. I kept this up 'til I tumbled down the basement stairs and hurt my back. Since she got the dog, Chloë could not get me to spend a single night in Harlem. Things got so bad that I even had a nightmare about that dog at home.

It came to me as I lay on the couch. It was about seven feet tall and it wore a gray trench coat that was open to display a naked, hairy, dog body and its erect purple manhood. The dog stood on his hind legs and bore down on me, but I fake him out, jump off the couch and flick on the light switch to make him disappear. I slept with every light on after that, but that action only seemed to illuminate the nightmares. I could recall them in chilling detail when I jumped up around two o'clock each morning, unable to return to sleep.

I couldn't go on with Chloë.

To leave, but where to go? To another dysfunctional situation? Home to live in my father house, when all my contemporaries had a house, car, mates, children and life and laughter?

Chloë was happy. She cooed, "Valdi, after your stunning display of ill will the first day you met Tennis, I didn't think you would be able to stay. What has it been ... three weeks? You have made great progress."

The dog did not stop glaring. My pills didn't stop dwindling. Although the psychologist cut down on my pills, the boy still had refills for his prescription. So I supplemented my prescription with extra doses of his. Fortified in this way, I was able to keep my issues with the dog on pause.

I read that poodles are supposedly sociable and generally like people. I bought it a toy squirrel and, once my feet were safely up on the recliner, I threw it in his direction. I swear that dog grabbed the squirrel and pelt it right back at me.

That same afternoon, after I had finished wiping the counter, I leaned over and filled his water bowl without thinking. That in itself was a shocker, but not as much as an eerie feeling of déjà vu that revived a similar memory over the water bowl of a big black dog.

The dog passed by the kitchen at this moment and see me with the jug still tipped towards its bowl. It ran in the kitchen and barked like I was caught in the act of tampering with his water. I slowly backed away from the counter. He walk past and nudged the water bowl with his nose until he had it jammed against a wall. Then he used his paw to turn it over.

That's when the war started. He knocked my iPod off the center table; chewed the strap off my handbag; peed in my box of newspapers and magazines on Barack Obama. He pulled down my clothes from the hangers in the boy's closet and made a bed of them. In the beginning I would tell Chloë about this canine terrorism but, from her expression, I knew she loved the dog best. Where to go? It was taunting me into leaving by just sitting and staring at me as I went about my daily routine.

On mornings, as I approached the stoop in Harlem, an iron bar would settle between my shoulders. I used to think the jumping and throbbing in my shoulder was bad, but toting an iron bar all day was infinitely worse. My head sprouted gray hairs like lawns sprout weeds. I start back walking backwards around the dog. I stop counting the pills.

I told Chloë that Cole was now well enough to return to school.

That way I could leave the house to the dog all day. Cole showed his glee by turning cartwheels so fast that he became a blur. He yelled breathlessly that he couldn't wait to show his latest trick to his friends, and Ava, Monica and Madam Lucian, too.

That evening, Chloë had brought in supper for the three of us. Long after the boy had said goodnight, we stayed up polishing off some wine. It was nearly eleven o'clock when I said goodbye, dismissing her entreaties to spend the night. Chloë turned in, and I went into the kitchen to put the glasses in the sink and give the counter a little wipe. Though I knew that dog was behind closed doors with the boy, I still walked backwards down the hall and across the foyer to the front door.

At the front door, I took off my house slippers and pushed my right foot in my shoe. Thunder clapped in my chest! I tried to kick the shoe off, but to no avail. I leaned on the wall, pull my foot up and used both hands to get the shoe off. The putrid smell of dog shit packed my nostrils. I hobbled around on my left foot, thrashing around for the bathroom. Meshed between my toes, under my toenails and in the deep fissures of my calloused heel was pasty, h-o-t dog shit. I tumbled into the foyer bathroom and, as I fumbled for the switch, I felt that dog brush past me in the dark. I slammed the door and, sitting there on the toilet bowl, I wept.

I wept, silently.

Hours later, I washed my foot in the face basin and emerged. The house was completely silent. I flung on the hall and kitchen lights. I refused to put on the one in the living room, because I just knew that dog was sleeping away on my red leather chair. I wiped his shit from the foyer and hallway walls. I tied up my shoe in a plastic bag for disposal, put on the house slippers and headed for home. Somewhere between Manhattan and Brooklyn, waiting at 3 a.m. for a train to show up, I decided it was me or the dog.

One day I almost keyed in "easy way to kill a dog for dummies," before I remembered that Internet surfing was saved and stored somewhere in the ether. Instead, I keyed in "protecting your pet from harmful substances." The Web delivered a whole list of pesticides and herbicides that could do dogs harm: lawn fertilizer, paint thinner, charcoal lighter fluid, rat poison and even chocolate. But I settled on anti-freeze because of that woman in the newspaper who had successfully arranged widowhood by stirring the stuff into her husbands' cocktails.

Though I had come up with a basic framework for the dog's end, I was paralyzed for weeks, because I couldn't discount the boy's feelings for the animal. It was that dog that had made him well. So I decided to give the dog a reprieve and just stay out its way. I dropped the boy off on mornings and then went to bookstores, museums, libraries, cafés ... anywhere I could rest my bones.

After I picked the boy up, I would take him to one of my old stomping grounds, the 72nd Street playground, as there was no reason to go by Sherman. Madam Lucian no longer had a job; Ava stopped going to the statue; and Uncle Ram stopped Monica from working and had moved her into his house because she was with child. I would bring the boy back home about six. That gave me an exact hour in the dog's company; enough time to bathe and feed Cole.

Chloë noticed how the dog slunk in the corners and bared his teeth at me. She laughingly remarked that the dog was jealous that I had kept the boy out all day. Since the night he shit in my shoe, the dog had taken full control over the red leather chair. He watched me straight in my face, his tail erect and stiff, and I understood clearly that that was a threat. The pills helped. I took the ones to help me relax; the ones that Chloë brought home for the pain in my back and Cole's refills. Only, now, I had to think through the smallest of acts – like how to take a step, and whether I should pee with the toilet seat up or down – before I did anything. I masked brandy with strong mints.

My resolve grew; I would kill the dog.

Once I had made the decision, he seemed to know, because he conceded the red chair and covered his face with his paw when I passed. He whimpered instead of growling, and chose to stay under Chloë's bed.

It would happen on a Monday.

Two Mondays passed before the right opening came. Chloë arranged a play date and dinner on the East Side that would bring us back to the house by 8:00 p.m. I didn't want the boy to see the dog put to sleep.

That Monday afternoon, shortly before we were due to leave, Cole came in the kitchen as I unpacked the dishwasher.

I said, "Feed the dog now, because we will be returning very late."

He adjusted the temperature in the water tap, filled the water bowl and put it carefully in its usual spot. He took down the box of dog crackers, selected three and arranged them on the dog's saucer. He climbed onto the counter and my heartbeat raced; I needed him to select canned dog steak for my plan to succeed. It was like watching a thriller in slow motion.

I held my breath. He picked up dry dog food, changed his mind and reached to the back of the cupboard and selected dog steak.

The can whirled around the opener until it crashed on the countertop. Two clumps in the bowl, a turn in the microwave, a last supper complete.

"Look at your face. Go wash it and let's go."

"I washed it yesterday."

I pointed down the hall. "And brush yuh teeth, too."

"But I'm going to get Tennis."

"It's still early, he will come when he's ready."

He stomped off, leaving the dog bowl on the counter. I followed him to the bathroom. He slammed the door in my face. I ran back to the kitchen, opened my pocketbook and pulled out the anti-freeze I had stored in an old, face-cream jar. I stared at the blue, liquid poison, but didn't feel nothing but shit between my toes. I poured.

Not a bubble, no reaction. The anti-freeze settled at the bottom of the bowl like blue soup.

No wonder the woman from the newspaper had chosen to put the damn anti-freeze in her husband's cocktail and not in his supper. It was better served in liquid.

I picked up the bowl with a paper towel, tipped the blue soup over the steak and drained the excess into the sink. I wiped the outside of the dog bowl with a wet cloth to protect Cole. The whirr of the toothbrush stopped. I pushed the paper towel in my pocketbook and sat by the kitchen table. The boy came in with the dog in his arms. He put it down and picked up the bowl of food from the counter.

"No. Don't give him that food," I said, springing over to the counter. The dog's ears lay flat against its head, its lips pulled back over its teeth. It bit into the air and the boy backed away.

"You're weird," the boy said holding the bowl above his head. Fearful that he would spill the contents, I took my seat again and watched as Cole presented the bowl to the dog. He stroked his fur as it ate and licked the bowl.

Once the dog was finished, the boy and the dog ran playfully out of the kitchen. I put on gloves and washed the bowl, relieved that the poisoning had gone very smoothly, without even a hint of drama.

NOT LIKE WHEN it happen before to my own dog, Lassie.

My Lassie! My own, nice, no-teeth, *pot hound* that would walk the two miles to school with me every day. Delia walked, too, but Lassie always stayed on my side. Once I had disappeared through the school gate, she turned around and headed home. Without fail, she would be waiting in the 2:00 p.m. sun to walk me back home.

Lassie's breast exploded one day. Papa and Aunty whispered cancer. Lassie could barely walk anymore because her maggot-filled breast almost touched the ground. She would lick me good-bye in the front yard. She never licked Delia. I couldn't concentrate at school, because I wanted to be home with Lassie, to salve her wound with handpicked cotton, a little black disinfectant and a hair-pin to take out the maggots. Then I would cuddle in the kennel with my nondescript, black, pot hound that had been with the family before I was even born. Papa said she had been named after an English Collie that used to be on television.

One day, Papa said, "Coop the chickens and turkeys, latch the pig pen tight, tie the goats, and lock up the dogs, except Lassie."

He dishes out cooked-up fish skin and rice into Lassie's bowl, and put it to cool on the banister. Fish is Lassie favorite food. No longer able to climb stairs, she sits on the bottom step staring up at the food, whimpering impatiently. When it has cooled enough, Papa tells me to take the bowl down to the yard for Lassie. I stand behind her stroking her fur as she eats. Her body stiffens and jerks. She looks back at me, her eyes imploring, "What have you done?" A gunshot goes off in my head. Lassie falls sideways in slow motion.

"Lassie! Lassie!" I am screaming into her brown eyes, closing her mouth to stop her blood from spewing. "Lassie, Lassie," I whim-pered, pushing my heartbeat into her shuddering body. Papa pulls me off.

"Come gyrl, wash yuh hands."

"Something happen to Lassie. Daddy, Lassie deading!"

"Valdina West, come wash dat poison off yuh hands before it land in yuh mouth. Leave de dawg; it done dead arready."

Papa leans me over the washtub and scrubs my hands with

blue, carbolic soap. He picks up the remainder of Lassie food, ties it into a bag and disappears out the front gate. The penned animals cry. I raise Lassie's lifeless head and put it on my lap. Her blood runs like a river over my yellow dress with the eyelet lace that came years ago from Aunty and Uncle in England. I bury my head in her neck.

"I sorry, Lassie. I sorry. I didn't mean it," I wail, but her eyes refuse to open, or even close.

"What have you done?" they accuse, over and over again.

I drop her head and bawl, the sounds coursing through the length and breadth of my body. I could see neighbors' mouths moving as they put their arms around me, but I couldn't feel or hear nothing in the darkness. Somebody fetches Papa who comes back cussing, mouth stink with rum. He drops Lassie into a *crocus bag* and sends her crashing into the back of a pick-up truck. She would go to the river for her rotting carcass to be poked with sticks by idle boys.

I raise my head. I was no longer a six-year-old in a dusty yard, but an old lady of forty-five in somebody's gleaming, silver kitchen. This time, Papa wasn't responsible for the blood on my yellow dress; the blood on my hands was my doing.

AUTUMN

I dialed Ava's phone over and over again, but she didn't answer. I had to know if those images of me poisoning a dog back home were actual memories or part of the hallucinations she had warned me about. She did not answer.

I took the boy around the corner to Fuzzy Burger and let him eat junk.

He asked me, "Why are you crying?"

It was then that I noticed water collecting on the lid of my sweet tea. I said my head was hurting, and he suggested that we cancel the play date and go back home.

I wanted to take the dog to the vet, but that was like ordering a jail cell. I pick up my tea, and me and the boy walked aimlessly through Harlem, with me not caring if the whole population of African-Americans feel I shouldn't be minding a white boy. Cole complained that he was cold. Though it was barely November, the temperature hovered around 35 ° F. We went to the library where I set him up on a computer. I went outside and dialed Ava again. She still didn't answer. I called Monica, who ambushed the call with a five-minute monologue that, given the amount of times she used that phrase, could well be titled, "Dat asshole, Uncle Ram." Monica was upset because Uncle Ram had sent for her children without consulting her.

"Valdi, I 'appy that my children ah come. But that's not the point. Uncle Ram do that to tie me down."

"Monica, okay, okay. Uncle Ram is an asshole, but I didn't call to talk about that. The boy's dog drink anti-freeze on the road."

"Well dat ah good news for you; him sure to dead. Remember a story you ah show us about a woman who kill two 'usbands with anti-freeze? You think I should give Uncle Ram some?"

"Monica, this is serious. I want you to check the Web to see what medicine would stop the dog from dying."

"Dat asshole, Uncle Ram, him ah cancel the Internet access 'pon my phone so I cyant go 'pon the Web. Anyway gyrl, I nah stay too long, my 'usband nah like to come 'ome and find me 'pon the phone. But, Valdi, call soon. These days you nah pick up at all."

"Just call; I will answer," I said, hustling up the library steps to google the cure for myself.

I sat on the opposite side of the room from the boy and selected a search engine. I key in: *"How to cure anti-freeze poisoning in animals."* The suggestion come back: *Vodka and a bicarbonate solution administered intravenously, approximately six hours after the poisoning, once the dog no longer looks drunk but before it begins to perform acrobatics. The antidote must be administered in this extremely small window when the dog appears normal to the human eye.*

Next, I key in: *What is a bicarbonate solution?* The answer come back: $NaHCO_3$. I pondered on the formula for a minute, then my pencil moved swiftly across the page. $CO_2 + 2NaOH \rightarrow Na_2CO_3 + H_2O$: *Baking Soda*. The ease with which I broke that down reminded me why I had had a hard time deciding whether I should pursue an undergraduate degree in science or literature. I was just too good at everything.

I had four hours to kill before the dog would appear "normal to the human eye." So I took the boy to the play date. When he was settled, I went hunting for a liquor store to buy the vodka. I had enough baking soda in the fridge.

WHEN WE OPEN the door to the brownstone, the dog did not greet the boy. I looked around, but only came up with a pool of vomit, which I cleaned immediately. The boy's giggles drew me to the bathroom where the dog was drinking water from the toilet. I ordered the boy to do his homework. Calmly, I picked up the dog and took it to the kitchen.

I was now within the window for administering the antidote because, when I rest the dog on the kitchen table, it didn't look drunk and it didn't try to do acrobatics. His obvious thirst presented the only opportunity to deliver the antidote by mouth, since I had no way of hooking him up to an IV.

I put him back on the floor. He panted over his water bowl as I mixed three tablespoons of baking soda in three cups of water with three tablespoons of vodka. I poured a shot glass of vodka for me and took a big sip. I didn't feel for it, so I emptied the rest into the dog's bowl. The dog gulped without sniffing, but when the taste hit him, he ran back to the bathroom door, scratching and whimpering. He backtracked to the bathroom in the hall and found that closed. He checked every bathroom in the house, but I was ahead of him. He returned to his bowl and licked it dry. I stood over him and poured as much water as he wanted into his bowl. Finally, he crawled under the red chair and went to sleep.

When Chloë returned, I didn't leave immediately. I had to mind the situation carefully. I sat in the kitchen chatting. When she realized I wasn't in a hurry, she asked if I minded if she went out. She took about an hour to change. Just as she was saying goodbye, the dog somersaulted from below the chair, landed on the dining table and jumped clear across the room. He crouched like a cat, then crawled on his belly until he reached my feet. He rolled away on his back, wagging his head. Chloë laughed. She said she was sorry the boy was asleep and missed the dog's tricks.

I couldn't bear to watch; I locked myself in the boy's room until silence came. I laid him on the red chair, where he drew his last breath. Chloë didn't notice anything untoward until Tuesday morning. She greeted me with the news at the door, and said that she was taking the day off to make funeral arrangements. She said it sheepishly, fully expecting me to say something sarcastic. I said that that was better than pelting the dog into the Hudson River.

Chloë said that I didn't have to attend if I wasn't into it, but a murderer always stays close to the crime scene, so I went. To my amazement, it was a real funeral with a big picture of the dog on an easel at the altar. The dog's coffin was sealed. He was cremated, and his ashes went back to the house in an urn.

I poured myself into the family after that. The boy get sick again. I feel bad. I feel shame. I feel guilty that I had done to Cole what had been done to me. Nothing was too big for me to do for that family after that. I walked away from my apartment in Brooklyn, taking only my clothes, and took up residence in Harlem. I refused Chloë's attempts at extra-compensation. I would leave the house only if forewarned that the boy's father was coming.

One day, he appeared without warning with another black poodle that was a dead ringer for the old one. The boy slammed it into the bathtub and ran away weeping. I sat on the edge of the tub and rocked the frightened little thing in my lap. The man come in the bathroom and jumped when he caught sight of us.

"Shit, I thought you were afraid of dogs."

A FRIDAY AFTERNOON found me dozing in the red chair 'cause I had to sleep when the boy did. The house phone rang on my lap. To my surprise, it was Ava.

"Valdi?"

Answering between sleep and wake like that closed the distance created from months of not speaking.

"What's up, gyrl?"

"Valdi, why is your cell phone disconnected? Put the TV on NY1, right now."

The remote dropped from my hand twice. I had never heard this tenor in Ava's voice. She keeps saying hurry up, but the TV was real old, so the volume came on way before the picture. A reporter was describing something that had happened in the Flatbush section of Brooklyn where foul play was not suspected. The screen blinked several times before settling on a five-inch window; a frame barely large enough to capture the police tape screening off the area in front of a Chinese restaurant.

"Ava, what's going on?"

"Shhhhh."

"Tell us about the Flatbush Bread Lady," says the reporter. At that precise moment, the TV screen shimmered and buzzed with "snow;" the sound becomes distorted and the tiny square disappears. I get up and bang the TV. I hear the tail-end of Monica's voice responding to the reporter, a cereal commercial, and Ava calling out my name. My voice is lost.

MRS. SHU, Ava and I hold up Monica in front the restaurant. The police tape gone, but candles, poems and loaves and loaves of bread pile up high. Mrs. Shu tell us that she going home. She knew black folks not crossing that altar for chicken wings and French fries.

The three of us sat at a bar next door. Over soda and between sobs, Monica say that she hadn't heard from Madam Lucian in two days. She rubbed her belly that fit snugly into her lap.

"She always called to ask if the baby kicking, if I ah eat good, how the children ah cope in America. So when me see days ah come and gawn, I ask Uncle Ram to bring me 'ere, to 'er place. When the door ah open ...."

"Monica, what happened when you opened the door?" Ava prodded gently.

"She was 'pon de bed dressed from 'at to shoe. 'Er 'ands fold and stiff cross she chest wid 'er Rosary beads wrap 'round dem. She look like she done in a coffin already."

Ava asked Monica a question I knew not to ask.

"So why yuh didn't call Valdi or me to say you couldn't find her, so we could come with you?"

"I'll repeat the last words that Madam Lucian said 'bout onno. She ah say dat the two ah onno mind only concerned with onno affairs."

Monica paused. "I tell 'er that this is America, and so it is sometimes.

"Ah true. Still, Valdi, ah where you ah hide? Did I tell you that Uncle Ram arrange to bring meh children up 'ere without me know 'til last minute? Him ah bring dem to control my movements, but still me ah glad to see dem. Now me nah send no more barrel ah clothes and toys to Jamaica for me sister to tief fi she pickney dem. Ava, I know your uncle mus' ah tell you 'bout the children, but me couldn't find you meself to tell you. Me and Madam Lucian called and called after yuh graduation party. We knock 'pon yuh door. We check 72nd Street playground before we ah decide to leave you alone."

I asked Monica if she know what kill Madam Lucian. She dipped in her pocketbook and pull out an empty medicine container that make me feel for my purple pills. Monica said if she didn't know better, she would think that Madam Lucian overdose 'cause the bottle was full with pills about four days ago.

"Me nah show *Babylahn* dis. Me ah push it inna me pocket before me ah even call dem. Me nah want dem to come to the wrong concluzahn. Besides, she nah have no reason to take her life," Monica say.

Madam Lucian had died without telling Monica that there was no house. She had left me as custodian of a secret that gave her all rights to put the damn pill bottle to her head. Ava looked confused. I could see her mentally running through her list of indicators to determine posthumously whether or not Madam Lucian had suffered from SIGECAPS. Yes, maybe it was Madam Lucian who had SIGECAPS all along, and her death was Ava's failure to see that. Ava put her head on the table for a long time. Monica patted her back, and I said that it look like we didn't really know how Madam Lucian was feeling under the mask she presented.

Monica pounded the table.

"I have been Madam Lucian friend and daughter and she nah wear no mask! Nobody should feel that she ah tek her own life!"

Both of them looked at me expectantly.

But there is no house. There never was!

I looked from Monica to Ava and remembered how I had stumbled upon the carcass of Madam Lucian's dream that day by Sherman, its blood still warm on the betrayer's knife. I wished that I, too, could have remained staring in wonderment at the unusual end of the happy, bread lady; her remains in a morgue somewhere.

I decided to let Dorothé leave with her secret intact. I must have muttered something, or maybe my warring emotions showed on my face.

Ava asked softly, "Valdi, is there something that we should know?"

Didn't they deserve to know? Monica's eyes begged me to allow her to keep her bond with Madam Lucian unbroken.

"Valdi, what do you know?" Ava pressed.

"I was just thinking that she didn't get to live in her fancy house, so we better give her a fancy casket."

The talk switched from "how come?" to the easier question of "what now?" Ava said that we had to contact Boyo before we go making plans, in case he want us to ship the body home or come up for the funeral. Monica phoned repeatedly but, of course, she couldn't reach him.

The next time we met was at Madam Lucian's apartment. We pulled four chairs around the kitchen table like old times, and sat on our usual seats. I lit a candle in front of Madam Lucian's empty spot. Monica fetched the money from under the floorboard and put it on the table.

"Almost nine thousand dollars," Ava said. We sat there and worked the phones, making arrangements to give Madam Lucian a great send off. The funeral home asked what we wanted on the tombstone. Ava opened a little poetry book she had to the first page. "We will put this," she said:

> The right to make my dreams come true I ask, nay, I
> demand of life, Nor shall fate's deadly contraband
> Impede my steps, nor countermand.

Monica said that was too much English for she, and Madam Lucian would not like that. To settle the argument I told them to blindfold me, and I would sit on Madam Lucian's chair and open the poetry book and point. That way, Madam Lucian get to decide. When the verse was picked every one grew quiet. I could hear Madam Lucian whispering that the message on her tombstone was for me too.

Bread for brick, Valdi. I looked at the others wondering if they had heard her too.

Madam Lucian's parish refused to give her the Mass of Christian Burial because the death certificate reflected the toxicology report. So, we kept our dead private. The day of the funeral, Ava picked Monica and me up in a limo, which had been "lovingly provided," she said sarcastically, by the people she works for. It was the first time she had mentioned them since we reunited.

At the funeral home, we sat in a tiny room with Madam Lucian laid out less than four feet away from us. It was surprising that, with all the bread Madam Lucian had sold, not *one* person showed up besides us. In the Caribbean, somebody like Madam Lucian would have had a big, *maco* funeral. We talked about good times by Sherman, the friggin', untouchable siboa, and Sunday morning breakfasts. Monica's memories pre-dated those of Ava and mine, and she shared them movingly. It was Madam Lucian who had best explained to her that going from mister to mister was no way to make a good future for herself. She walked over to the casket and laid her head on Madam Lucian chest. My heartbeat skipped because Monica belly was big and new death and new life wasn't supposed to mix up like that!

Ava helped me lead Monica back to her chair, and we spent the next half-hour listening to the funeral home chaplain talking about somebody he didn't know. The six somber pallbearers, costing two hundred and fifty dollars each, hoisted Madam Lucian on their shoulders and we followed them to the hearse. As the door clicked gently behind Madam Lucian, Monica hugged the hearse and wept.

Uncle Ram had warned Monica not to take *his* belly to the cemetery. That meant Monica had to be taken home before the interment. Ava told the hearse driver to go slow, and directed the limo driver to Monica's house. Monica implored Ava to talk to Uncle Ram about his controlling ways. Ava agreed, but told Monica not to expect a change.

"That's why he had no wife when you met him. I warned you to keep it strictly business. A Green-Card marriage is a Green-Card marriage, Monica. There is no pleasure in that."

Ava and I rode in silence as the limo sped through the back roads to Cypress Hills Cemetery. We arrived just as Madam Lucian's casket, strapped to a metal rack, began its lonely descent into the earth.

"Wait!" Ava and I shouted, jumping from the doors on either side of the limo. A lone grave worker in a red bandana jumped as we approached.

"Ava, I'm sure she didn't even get one prayer here, not one," I said.

To my great surprise, Ava garbled something softly in what I presumed to be Hindi, her voice growing more confident as she chanted. The grave worker removed his bandana and clutched it to his chest. Together, we listened to Ava's sorrowful poem.

"I prayed that her soul would be transformed from *preta* to *pitrs*: spirit to ancestor," she explained.

I told her that Madam Lucian would have liked that because she believed in all prayers. Ava laughed, "Well she still waiting to hear an 'amen' pass your lips. You could say it today," she said.

"Okay. Amen." I said. "You hear dat, Madam Lucian? Amen for you!"

The gravedigger asked if he could send Madam Lucian down. As he retied his bandana. I stepped onto a mound of dirt to drop a rose on the casket. Instantly, I see myself walking up a dusty road to the Catholic Church on the hill on my way to Sister Catherine's funeral.

Caskets didn't open all the way in those days. A circle of glass over Sister Catherine's face protected the living from the dead, and the dead from the living. I had said "amen" freely that day, after a long string of prayers.

"Eternal rest grant unto her, O Lord, and let perpetual light shine upon her. May she rest in peace. Amen."

Those same words tumbled out for Madam Lucian. A real Catholic prayer from the Mass of Christian Burial, which I repeated over and over. Ava said it, too.

Way back when, we had said it about one hundred times for Sister Catherine, and she was a nun. Ava and I said it more than that for Madam Lucian, because she was a saint.

"May the souls of all the faithfully departed, through the mercy of God, rest in peace. Amen," the gravedigger added when we trailed off. He peddled Madam Lucian down gently; dirt filled the hole.

"How are things at your job?" Ava say.

"The boy not well. He had a dog, and it died."

Another time, she would have wanted to know what the hell I had been doing there with a dog, but that was then.

I looked at Ava, really looked at her. She had her coat pulled tightly across her chest. It was all she could do to keep from biting her nails. She told me it was really goodbye.

"I know. Even though the grave right there it's hard to believe she gone."

"Ah talking 'bout me," Ava say. I paid attention, because she was talking slang.

She looked young and small; weak and unembellished; she looked so ... Indian. Little Vasumati from Guyana *backdam,* before Prada.

"Valdi, this is the last time you will see me."

Back home in Trinidad, we use to call weed killer "Indian tonic," so I asked Ava to explain what she meant by "goodbye."

"Ava, ah here, if you want to say something, unburden yuhself, I will listen." She squeezed my hand.

"Goodbye simply means ah going home to Guyana."

Loss that began with Madam Lucian, and Monica to some extent, caused my chest to tighten. I drew deep breaths as four journeys unravelled into one. I was now officially alone on my path, heart on the ground.

"Oh Gawd, Ava. Why?"

She shrugged.

"Did you tell your family?" Her hands shook.

"You plan to say anything? When yuh leaving?"

"Ah not taking de limo back with you. I going directly to the airport. I will reach Guyana before nightfall."

She shifted from foot to foot, "Oh Valdi, I'm leaving as I came."

Her body heaved and racked, but her face remained tearless because, inside, she was crying blood.

"Was all for naught, Valdi. All for naught. You was right about dem."

She hugged and let me go in the same instant, then turned in the direction of the road.

"Ava, I was not right," I hear myself say.

Feelings churned into words about love and kindness, patience and pride. Humility. Tolerance. It was why I had been stuck in a rut. I had taken too long to understand the message of my condition. In a blinding instant I understood why, despite Uncle Ram, Monica's story would turn out the best. It was because she always kept it real. I couldn't stop Ava from leaving, but I held her tight hoping to give her something for the road — some mustard seed of hope and wisdom that she would always remember me for.

"Valdi, don't make this harder," Ava said.

"Gyrl, you will make it. You will make it because you are the strongest person I know. You have done good for yourself and for people, including me. Ava, you will make it because you educated, and you'll be in your own country."

Ava broke free and scurried past the limo, down the hill framed by tombstones, until she blew like a speck out the gate.

MADAM LUCIAN'S PLOT was nice and smooth; the flat marble tombstone wedged firmly in the earth. I stepped back to the grave to check on things. In hindsight, we should have gone with Monica's suggestion to select an upright tombstone even if it didn't come in lavender. More people would have seen it as they trudged by to bury their own dead.

Slowly, softly, I said her name: the real one that was carved into the tombstone. I recognized the date she came and the date she left. Almost fearfully, I recalled those prophetic words that had come to us when I, in blindfold, had touched a verse in Ava's book of poetry. She had used me, the involuntary keeper of her secret, as her medium to make known her final wishes. I crouched to read the inscription.

DOROTHÉ (M. L.) ALCINDORE
December 4, 1934 – November 10, 2008

Too long my heart against the ground
Has beat the dusty years around,
And now, at length, I risė, I wake!
And stride into the morning break!
(Georgia Douglas Johnson, *Calling Dreams*)

Change had come for Madam Lucian. Change had come for Monica. Change had come for Ava.

•

I straightened up and inhaled deeply as the gray mist approaches. In the silence of the graveyard I heard Madam Lucian whisper, "Bread for brick, Valdi. Bread for brick." In a flash of clarity, I refused the fog and saw life, Oh, life, roiling with possibilities.

THE END

Glossary

all skin teeth is not grin. Things are not always what they seem.

Babylahn. Variation of "Babylon": Jamaican slang for the police.

bacchanal. Good party; rowdy or scandalous behavior.

bacchanal talk. Mindless banter and gossip with possibly sexual overtones.

backdam. Caribbean usage: Originally, an area beyond the plantation fields used by laborers to grow crops; rural and unsophisticated.

Bajan. Barbadian.

Banga seed. A type of palm tree whose fruit contains an extremely hard seed.

Base good. Get really covered in something.

boldface. Brazen.

boop. Onomatopoeic spelling to describe something or someone falling with a thud.

buck up'pon. To come upon someone or something unexpectedly.

buckra. A disparaging name used to describe a "white person" in charge.

burqa. Arabic: An enveloping outer garment worn by women in some Islamic countries.

chirren. Children.

coating. Covering something or someone completely.

commonness. Crass behavior.

corbeau. French: A black carrion crow, a vulture.

corbeaux. French: The plural form of corbeau, carrion crows or vultures.

couya mouth. A signal made by pushing the lips together and using them to point silently at something or someone.

crocus bag. Variation of burlap bag.

cuss me out. Tell me off.

cut eye. An insolent and cross look that involves looking at someone from head to toe and vice versa to show extreme annoyance.

cut her teeth. Begin a new undertaking

dadder head. A derogatory term for hair of coarse texture.

Dan Dadda. The head honchos in an organization.

done the talk. End the conversation on a given topic.

dress rong. Move over.

duppy. An evil spirit.

dust dis bwoy bottom. Clean the seat of the boy's pants with one's hands.

dutty. Dirty.

everlasting. Humongous.

faked out. Dodged.

friggin'. A polite swear word; variation of the word "fucking."

frizzle fowl. A breed of chicken with curly feathers that displays skittish behavior while brooding.

fronting. Pretending.

Garifuna. An ethnic group of mixed Carib and African ancestry who live primarily in Central America.

ginch. To flinch guiltily when caught out or to react defensively to an anticipated blow.

gwan. Go on.

haunted. Restless, agitated.

ha ya yie. An expression of disgust or mental anguish that is real or imagined.

h-o-t. Pungent, stinking to high heaven.

I just dey. I'm just here, doing nothing special; chilling.

It's the change from the dollar that makes the noise. It's the reaction to an action that escalates the situation.

jamet. A lady of ill-repute or loose morals.

jamming. Dancing.

jouvay. Pre-dawn masquerade festivities that officially open the Trinidad and Tobago carnival parade that begins before dawn.

jumbie. A spirit that frightens or terrorizes the living.

liming. Hanging out with friends, having fun and fervent discussions.

maco. An event so excessive as to set tongues gossiping.

maga. Meager, scrawny.

making monkey face. Pulling funny faces.

malcady. Tremors in the body; similar to having an epileptic seizure.

mouth plates. Dentures.

niggler. A feeling in the back of one's mind that's trying to prompt recall of a memory.

nine-night ceremony. A ceremony of passage, where friends meet to give comfort and support to the relatives of the deceased and to wish the departed a safe journey to life's next stage.

obeah. Afro-Caribbean shamanism.

ole talk. Idle chatter.

onno rass nonsense. Your ridiculous discussion(s).

onno. You (plural), your.

oomph. Aura.

pan side. A steel-pan orchestra.

peeny. Tiny.

pot hound. Mongrel, mixed breed of dog.

praps. The onomatopoeic sound of a heavy weight dropped from a height to the floor.

rass. Variously translated as "hell," "ridiculous," or "ass."

red bamsee chimpanzee. Refers loosely to the antics of a baboon whose hind parts become a reddish colour when it is ready to breed.

roti. A type of flatbread normally eaten with curries or cooked vegetables.

sawatee. Big shot.

siboa. Dried cassava.

sipped a little bush tea for his fever. Defended his rights without being asked to.

skinned and grinned. Pretended to make nice, especially in the face of uneven odds.

slack. Lacking in decorum.

smelling agouti in the woods. Smelling a rat; becoming suspicious.

so-so. Barely tolerable.

soucouyant. A Trinidadian vampire, usually in the guise of an old woman in daylight, that sheds its human skin and flies at night as a ball of fire to suck the blood of its victims while they sleep.

soused. Drenched; overcome by emotion.

standing. Status.

steeeeeeuuuuups. A sibilant sound made by sucking air into one's mouth and letting it flow over the sides of the tongue while it is pressed up against the hard palate; meant to convey disgust; the longer the sound, the deeper the disgust.

sucked my teeth. Made the steeeeups sound.

Sunday food. A set Sunday lunch in Trinidad and Tobago of meat, callaloo, macaroni pie, peas or beans, rice, potato salad, boil plantains and sweet potato.

sweet-eye. Wink.

take a taste. To drink some rum or other type of alcohol.

take in front. To pre-empt someone else's action by acting first.

wan. One, alone.

wan woman. A woman.

wash their mouth on me. Say bad things about me.

washing wares. Doing the dishes.

water-mouth. Gossipy, indiscreet person.

when water drowned flour. When adversity multiplied and overcame the good times.

yampee. Mucus found in the corners of the eyes after a long night's sleep.